MW00577195

ACCIDENTALLY YOURS

ALEXA RIVERS

Copyright © 2019 by Alexa Rivers

Accidentally Yours

All rights reserved.

No part of this book may be reproduced in any form or by any electronic or mechanical means, including information storage and retrieval systems, without written permission from the author, except for the use of brief quotations in a book review.

This book is a work of fiction. All people, places, organizations and events contained within it are figments of the author's imagination, or creative license has been used.

Cover by Shannon Passmore at Shanoff Designs

To Kayne.
For supporting me one hundred percent
while I explore the world in my head.

CHAPTER 1

*A*ria Simons hovered just inside her boss, Derek's, office, fidgeting with the hem of her shirt. Derek had summoned her and her colleague Johnny Chen, the sports reporter for the *South Canterbury Chronicle*, to his office a few minutes ago with no explanation. It made her nervous. Aria loved her job reporting on local community issues and generally sailed under the radar, avoiding contact with upper management. In her last job, appearing too friendly with management had gotten her in trouble, and she'd been determined not to repeat her previous mistakes when she started at the *Chronicle*.

Johnny leaned against the doorframe beside Aria, both of them uncomfortable being singled out by Derek, who looked totally in control, poring over tomorrow's articles behind his massive oak desk. He hadn't glanced up since they entered, although he knew they were there. Power play. How Aria hated it.

Finally, he raised his head. "Miss Simons, Mr. Chen, thank you for coming. You may have heard that Kaia Anglem has resigned."

Aria shook her head and glanced at Johnny, who seemed equally surprised. "When does she leave?"

"Four weeks. She handed in her letter yesterday. She's moving to the *Christchurch Press*."

Aria clutched her stomach as it roiled uncomfortably. The *Press*. Even the name dredged up a host of unpleasant memories. Wilson Jones' creepy advances, the judgement, the censure. She prayed Kaia would be smarter than she'd been.

"She'll be missed," Johnny replied. He'd pushed off from his position against the doorframe and stood tall, his arms folded over his chest. "And she'll leave a real gap in the organization."

Ah, now she realized why they were here. The pain in her stomach fizzled out, replaced by excitement, and she fought to hide a grin. It wouldn't do to get ahead of herself.

"Exactly." Derek was smiling now. "I've spoken with the other editors, and they've nominated the two of you for promotion to Kaia's position as senior reporter."

"That's fantastic," Aria began, but Derek silenced her with a hand gesture.

"Unfortunately, as you see, there is one position and two of you."

Aria met Johnny's eyes and saw them narrow. As a natural athlete, being competitive was in his blood. In contrast, Aria had kept her competitive side under wraps since leaving the *Press*. She'd always thought of her Type A personality as an advantage, until suddenly it wasn't. Putting it behind her had taken a lot of effort, and she just knew Derek was about to bring it to the fore.

Derek slapped his palms down on the desk and leaned forward, his smile taking on an edge. "I will be reading all of your articles over the next four weeks, and whoever has stirred the most public interest at the end of that time will be given the promotion."

"Thank you for the opportunity," Aria said, pressing her palms together nervously. "I'm sure we'll both do our best."

This was it. Her chance for redemption.

Johnny nodded to her. "May the best man win."

∼

"WE NEED TO MEET. NOW."

Aria recognized the voice on the other end of the phone immediately. "Hello to you too, Eliza. What can I do for you?"

She'd called Eliza Brown and a few other contacts earlier, looking for a good story to start earning her promotion. Eliza had murmured something typically vague and hung up. One of two real estate agents based in Aria's hometown, Itirangi, Eliza was grey-haired and stern, reminiscent of a school headmistress—it certainly wasn't her bubbly personality or welcoming smile that sold houses. Eliza was efficient. Frighteningly so.

"I need to talk to you. I have some news you might be interested in."

Regardless of how desperate Aria was for a juicy story, she had a four o'clock deadline and two articles to finish. "Now doesn't suit. How about first thing tomorrow morning?"

"Now, Miss Simons." The words were sharp. In another life, Eliza Brown would have made an excellent drill sergeant. "It will be worth your while. Meet me at the bakehouse."

Aria glanced at her watch. Just past one o'clock. She could finish her stories at home and email them in. If Eliza's story could help her win a promotion, she'd be a fool to ignore her. "I'll see you soon."

. . .

NEW ZEALAND-FAMOUS for its award-winning pies and magnificent backdrop, Itirangi's bakehouse was built on a terrace above Lake Itirangi and looked out over an enormous body of azure water that stretched into the distance, ending at the foot of the Southern Alps. Suspended glacial sediments produced the rich blue of the lake. 'Itirangi' translated to 'Little Sky' in Te Reo, the language of the Maori people, and the reason for the name was obvious to anyone who visited on a fine day. For then, they would see a perfect reflection of the heavens upon the water.

Eliza was yet to arrive, but Aria's friend Emily Parker, the local florist, was sitting at a table by the window. Redheaded and lovely, Emily was Itirangi's businesswoman of the year. Aria took a seat next to her and checked the time. A full three minutes had passed since the last time she'd looked.

She turned to her friend. "Hey, Em."

"Hey there." Emily greeted her, looked up from the newspaper and grinned. "I'm just reading the article you wrote yesterday about the increase in local housing prices. Interesting stuff."

Aria grimaced. Human interest stories were her favorite; economics, not so much. "If you say so."

Emily returned to reading. Aria tapped her foot and wondered why she'd been called here. She *hated* not knowing. It was her mission in life to know everything, and to know it first. She called it journalistic instinct. Her friends called it nosiness.

Finally, Eliza arrived and took a seat across from her. She cleared her throat and rested her hands on the table. "Miss Simons, I'm sorry for being brief on the phone. I wanted to discuss this in person."

"You said you have a story for me?"

"I do." Eliza summoned a waitress and requested a pot of tea. "You're aware, of course, that an investor has purchased the remaining land at the Lakeview subdivision."

"Yes." It had been a major coup. Itirangi had once been owned entirely by locals, but within the last few years, out-of-towners had begun investing in holiday homes and accommodation businesses. Only a few weeks earlier, an unknown quantity had purchased the large property left over from a residential subdivision. The subdivision, on the top of a hill, had a clear view over the township to the lake, and the newly purchased block of land was a prime piece of real estate—too pricey for most locals.

"I've investigated the company who purchased the land and have some disturbing news," Eliza said. "They're planning to build a shopping complex and a motel."

Aria's eyes widened in surprise. Once a rural backwater, Itirangi was becoming a popular tourist destination thanks to its warm summers, gorgeous lake, view of the mountains and proximity to the ski fields. Despite that, it retained a small-town charm, and she hadn't imagined any commercial property developers would be seriously interested in it.

Boutique clothing stores, souvenir shops, and jewelers lined the main street. A shopping complex and an accommodation complex would mean competition for the local stores.

"Oh my god," Aria said. "Are you sure?"

"As sure as I can be. It's my understanding that the council received an application to build on the site this morning."

Eliza was right. This *was* a good story. A new shopping complex would change the atmosphere of Itirangi. "Surely, the councilors won't approve it. Something of this scale would mean a change of direction for the town."

Emily put aside her newspaper and interrupted. "They almost certainly will. Dad thinks it's a brilliant idea. From what I've heard, the other councilors are also on board. It'll create job opportunities and bring in more tourists. It was bound to happen eventually."

"But what about the existing businesses?" Aria asked. "A

new development will mean more competition for them."

"But it will also mean more variety for shoppers. They can see potential for an overall benefit to the town. Councilors Jackson and Reynolds plan to set up shop in the new premises."

"Which is why I called you." Eliza turned her black eyes on Aria, the corners of her mouth upturned. Some might say it was a smile, but Aria knew otherwise. Eliza never smiled. And if it was silly to be afraid of a little old lady, then Aria was a fool, because Eliza terrified her.

"Why, exactly?" she asked, dread bubbling in the pit of her stomach with the surety that Eliza hadn't invited her here purely to help her with a story.

"You have the power to ruin this company with bad publicity. Make it so difficult for them that they decide it's not worth building here. Turn public opinion against them."

"Public opinion will already be divided." As with all change, some people would think of it as an opportunity and some would resist.

"To a certain extent," Eliza agreed. "But no one outside of Itirangi realizes how special this place is the way it is. You can reach a wider audience than I can. People respect you, Miss Simons. They listen to what you have to say."

"I want a big story," Aria said. "I need one, and this could give me a whole mini-series, so thank you for that, but I won't set out to demonize the developer. If that's what comes of it, then so be it, but I'll go wherever the story takes me."

"Do whatever you can." Although Eliza's expression didn't change, Aria had a sense that Eliza was pleading with her. She had to set her straight. "*If* I write about this, I can't promise you what the outcome will be."

Eliza sighed. "It will have to do."

Closing her eyes, Aria sucked in a breath. Yes, this might just give her the story she needed, but Eliza's revelation had wider implications. When Aria returned home to Itirangi after eight years away, she'd envisioned weekends spent kayaking, swimming, or reading in the sun in her quiet backyard. The thought of major companies taking an interest in developing Itirangi had crossed her mind. How could it not, when property prices were soaring, and the hotels were constantly full? But, somehow, she'd convinced herself it wouldn't really happen. That Itirangi wouldn't become yet another bustling lakeside tourist town like Queenstown. Not that there was anything wrong with Queenstown, but it was a hive of activity. Aria preferred the laidback lifestyle of her hometown.

She felt sick to her stomach. Mouth dry, she pushed away from the table and stood. "I'll do some research tonight and should have something to publish in the next couple of days." Reaching over, she shook Eliza's hand, conscious that her own felt cold and clammy, then turned and strode toward the exit.

ELIJAH LOCKWOOD STALKED from one end of his Auckland-based office to the other, tracking a path across the lush carpet. Outside the window, the pinnacle of the Sky Tower stood prominently against the skyline.

"You told me we'd have the go-ahead a month ago," he barked to the foreman on the other end of the phone. The man was handling his latest development, in a hick town fast on its way to becoming a tourist hotspot. "I have a timeline to work to. Now I have to adjust it. I have tradesmen booked. Engineers and interior designers I'll have to reschedule. Remind me why we're having these problems."

"A few of the locals aren't cooperating," the foreman explained. "They're throwing up roadblocks wherever possible."

"Why?" Eli asked, beginning to pace again, forward

toward the window looking out over the central business district, then back to the dark mahogany desk. "And how many?"

"Just a handful. They're campaigning to 'keep it local'. Complaining that their businesses will lose customers."

Eli groaned and rubbed his temples. "This will be good for them. They're just too set in their ways to see it. What can I do to smooth things along?"

He wasn't generally a diplomatic person. Not charming or good at handling people. But he did have a talent for frightening them into submission. It wasn't his preferred tactic. He slept better at night when business was amicable, but he understood that scare tactics were sometimes necessary.

"Maybe you could come down here and deal with it yourself," the foreman suggested. "Conflict isn't really my thing."

Eli glanced at his calendar, which was booked full of meetings and appointments for the foreseeable future. No personal time, no time off. He hadn't dated in months, rarely saw his family, and had long since lost contact with all the friends who weren't also colleagues. He simply didn't have the time.

Massaging his temples again, he thought of the time and effort he'd put into this latest project. His decision to build in the small town was a first, but he'd done his research, and the tourism industry in Itirangi was growing exponentially. Dozens of wealthy men and women were purchasing holiday homes there, and the local accommodation was booked months in advance.

This investment would pay off in spades. The research said so, the numbers said so, and most importantly, his gut said so. Eli was a logical man, but he had a really good feeling about this, and he was willing to make sacrifices. Unfortunately, taking time away from his office in New Zealand's largest city was nigh on impossible.

"I'll think on it," he said. "In the meantime, do what you can."

~

THE REST of the afternoon passed quickly for Aria. She hammered out her stories and submitted them. Then she looked over property records for the Lakeview subdivision site and made a call to Hemi Densom. She needed to know exactly what this Lockwood Holdings company was proposing.

Hemi was a town planner. They'd been on a date once, but they were better friends than lovers. He was perfectly nice: funny, smart, and charming, and at six feet tall with broad shoulders, a swarthy complexion and dark hair, also pretty damn hot. But he didn't make her pulse quicken, give her butterflies or make her tongue trip over itself.

The call connected. "Hemi Densom speaking."

"Hi, Hemi," she said. "It's Aria here."

"Aria! *Kei te pehea koe?* How are you?"

"*Kei te pai au,*" she replied. "Better now that I'm talking to you."

"You smooth talker." He chuckled. "Did you ask someone for my number? Because I don't remember giving it to you." His voice dropped to a whisper. "Are you stalking me, Ri?"

"Nothing that exciting." Aria's tone was wry, her fingers crossed. "I'm hoping you might do me a favor."

"What kind of favor?" Hemi sounded wary. "You know that most of my work is confidential."

"I only want some public information," she assured him.

"You'll have to be more specific." His guard was up.

"Did you receive an application for a mall development in Itirangi?"

"Word spreads fast." Obviously, he'd discounted the town's penchant for gossip.

"Sure does. I'll take that as a yes. Can I get a copy of it?"

"You could have come to the council and asked at the front desk. Why call me?" Hemi's frustration was clear, even if she didn't know the reason for it.

"Then I wouldn't have had the pleasure of talking to you." She was laying it on a bit thick but couldn't help it. Hemi had a sarcastic sense of humor, as well as a natural irreverence, and he brought out the same in her.

"Not funny, Ri."

Sighing, she admitted the truth. "I was hoping to hear your opinion. You know, how it looks, whether it's likely to be approved. I've heard that the councilors support it."

"You know I can't tell you my opinion," he chastised her. "And who told you that the councilors support it?"

"Emily Parker."

"Councilor Parker talks too much," Hemi grumbled. "Emily isn't much better."

"Hemi!" Aria was shocked. Rude comments were a world away from what she'd come to expect from him. "Emily is lovely."

"Yeah, she is." He sighed. "*Aroha mai.* Sorry, it's been a rough day. Do you know how many people have knocked on my door today, wanting to know about this development?"

"A few," she guessed. No wonder he didn't want to talk about it.

"Eight," he said. "Five angry ratepayers who think we should dismiss the application without even considering it, and three who think it's the best thing since sliced bread."

"That's rough."

Hemi sighed again, and she could hear paper rustling in the background. "I'll email the application through to your work address. The most I can say is that they're complying with the council's standards for the building design."

"Thanks, Hemi. I really appreciate it."

CHAPTER 2

*E*arly the next morning, Eli sat behind his desk fiddling with a pen, brainstorming ways he could get the locals of Itirangi on-side for his development. Because, really, it should be obvious that the development would help them. But he was getting nowhere.

His personal assistant Joan stuck her head around the door. "Mr. Lockwood?"

He looked up, glad of the interruption. "What is it?"

"I think you should see this." She disappeared, and a moment later, called out, "Check your emails."

The email she'd forwarded to him had a link to a newspaper article entitled "Multi-million-dollar Development Threatens Local Businesses." As he skimmed the article, his blood pressure skyrocketed. Someone in Itirangi wanted to sabotage him. That was the only explanation. He looked for the journalist's by-line. Aria Simons. The headshot showed a pretty brunette. Of course the media wanted to twist his plans and make him bleed. That was what they did best. Ever since... He shook his head, dispelling the old memory. Victoria was past. The problem in Itirangi was present.

"Joan!"

"Yes, Mr. Lockwood?"

"Book me a flight to Christchurch, accommodation in Itirangi, and cancel my appointments for the rest of the week."

"Cancel your appointments?" she asked, her face blanching. "All of them?"

"Reschedule the appointments that can't be cancelled. Keep any phone appointments. Cancel the rest."

"Are you sure?" she asked, now white as paper.

"Yes. I think this situation needs a personal touch. I trust you can manage to shuffle everything around."

"Y-yes," she stammered, darting from the room before he could issue any more orders.

Eli gazed out of the window. Lockwood Holdings Limited, a prime piece of real estate in the heart of the city, was a testament to how far he had come. But there was so much left for him to do. And it started with Itirangi.

ARIA WRAPPED the camera cord around her wrist and strolled onto the Lakeview property, now owned by Lockwood Holdings Limited. It didn't have a driveway yet, and, courtesy of a long, hot summer, the grass was more brown than green. Technically, she wasn't allowed to be here, but, she'd reasoned, it couldn't hurt to pop over for a few minutes to take some photos. Maybe she could superimpose the concept plan of the shopping complex over a photo of the empty lot. Great photography equaled more attention to her article and, hopefully, a promotion. The response to her first article had been crazy. Whether people agreed with it or not, everyone had an opinion.

Flipping her sunglasses over her eyes to shield them from the sun, Aria looked down on Itirangi. Sometimes she wondered if it wouldn't benefit from an upgrade—a few more modern amenities. At the moment, the newer buildings stood out like scars on the landscape, while many of the older buildings were in need of painting, with tussocks in the gardens and scrub that grew unchecked. There was a certain wilderness about Itirangi. Aria thought it was beautiful. And, considering the booming tourist trade, she wasn't alone in her view.

She pondered her next story. She needed to provide the public with more details about the development. She'd done her research and now she was here, searching for inspiration. Wandering around the edge of the property, she snapped photos of the yard, then walked to the highest point and stood on tiptoes. She gazed out toward the lake, over the cottages with overrun lawns and the boutique shops in hundred-year-old buildings. The shimmering lake lapped at the shore. Behind the mass of water, mountains towered brown and green, blending into the horizon. It dazzled her. No wonder someone wanted to build in this spot. They would make a killing.

A sparrow swooped into a tree, and she shot a picture of it mid-flight. Perfect. She was certain one of these photos would be exactly what she needed to liven up her article. While tucking the camera away, she heard a scuffle. Peering over her shoulder, she jumped when she saw a man standing a few yards away. She took a quick step backwards and trod on a stick which rolled under her foot. Her legs gave out beneath her, and she landed on her bottom. *Dammit!* She cursed her clumsiness, a trait it seemed she'd never grow out of. Her butt throbbed. She looked up to introduce herself. And up. And up.

The man loomed over her. He pushed a hand through brown hair tipped with gold, his sky-blue eyes wide in disbelief which slowly turned to disdain as he peered down the length of his perfectly placed nose at her. His full lips pursed, exaggerating a cupid's bow. Five o'clock shadow dusted his cheeks, and his black coat and silk tie were impeccable. The dark colors complimented his golden skin. She couldn't help staring.

Who was he?

No one dressed like this in Itirangi. Even the businessmen wore casual clothes. Jeans and shirts. This man came from another world. A god among mere mortals, gorgeous enough to drive god-fearing women to sin.

$\sim$

ELIJAH WASN'T sure whether to be angry at having his peaceful night interrupted or intrigued by the woman at his feet. She had been standing tall at the end of the paddock, like a queen surveying her domain. Except, up close, she was less of a queen and more... Well, odd. Wearing an absurdly fluffy pink jersey with purple leggings, she'd presented her well-formed behind to him as he'd approached unnoticed. Now, she was sitting in the dirt with her hair falling over her face, peering up at him. How bizarre.

He felt a brief flash of sympathy, but it was tempered by annoyance. It had been a long day, and he'd had enough. Not a people-person at the best of times, when he was tired, he preferred to be alone.

Reluctantly, he reached down to help her up. She laid a small, warm hand in his. "Are you okay?" he asked.

"Fine," she replied, her cheeks flushing a delicate shade of pink. "Thanks."

She flicked her long dark hair as she straightened, the curls corkscrewing over her shoulders. Several inches shorter than he, she squinted up into his face, wrinkling her small, upturned nose. Her eyes were brown with flecks of green that flared as she held his gaze. The woman was prettier than he had imagined based on the outlandish outfit.

"What were you doing?" he asked.

"Taking photos." She gestured helplessly at the camera that was still on the ground where she'd fallen. She knelt to pick it up, her leggings tightening over her butt.

"There are better viewpoints of the lake," he told her. This was a nice spot, to be sure. That was why he'd bought it. But there were plenty of nice lookouts much easier to access near the lakefront.

"I know that," she replied indignantly. "I'm a local."

Eli raised an eyebrow. She looked vaguely familiar. "Then, why the camera?"

She glanced away. "I'm doing some research for an article. I work for the paper."

"Look at me."

She started at his sudden command, and her eyes went to his. He jolted in recognition. She was the journalist who'd written that blasphemous article, without a doubt. What the hell was she doing here?

"Did you know this is private land?" he asked, willing to give her the benefit of the doubt this once.

"I know," she admitted with an impish smile. "You won't tell on me, will you?"

He looked up at the sky, jaw clenched. Did she have another awful article in the works? What had he done to deserve this? He tugged on a handful of hair and lowered his gaze back to her. "Tell who, Miss Simons?" he asked. "You've already told on yourself. I'm Elijah Lockwood. This is my property."

"How do you know my name?" she demanded. Then she paled. "*Lockwood*?" She seemed to pull herself together and stuck out a hand. "Nice to meet you. I'm Aria Simons."

"I know," he said impatiently. "You're the journalist who's trying to ruin me."

Her jaw dropped. "I'm not trying to ruin you. I don't know why you'd think that."

"Your bleeding-heart article in yesterday's paper. It wasn't exactly open-minded."

"It wasn't untrue, either," she said, eyeing the exit as if she were considering making a run for it. "I presented one side of the argument. Not the only side."

Eli wanted to rail at her. Could he not get a break? His day had been long enough without adding reporters to the mix.

"You'll print a retraction in tomorrow's paper," he said firmly.

The reporter bristled. Her spine straightened, and her eyes gleamed. "I'm working on a series of articles, Mr. Lockwood, and there's a lot riding on it." He snorted derisively, and her eyes flashed before she continued, "I'll write about every aspect of this development, but I'll do it in my own time, and I'll certainly not print a retraction. I'm not ashamed of my work."

He scowled and crossed his arms. "Suit yourself. There are other ways to fix the problems you've made."

"Look." When she took hold of his arm, her nearness overwhelmed him. His palms started sweating, and he tucked them more firmly into the crooks of his elbows. Did she not understand personal boundaries? "I haven't been trying to make problems for you," she said. "I'm only doing my job. Your development is big news around here. We're a small community, so you shouldn't have expected anything else."

Eli supposed she was right. She had a job to do, and so did he. Clearly, she wasn't going to be as cooperative as he'd hoped. Not that he should have expected anything else. The media hadn't treated him kindly in the past. Never mind. He'd find another way.

Eli's gaze wandered down her body. She was slim but rounded in all the right places, and her body was nicely displayed by the tight, bright clothes. His fingers tingled with the desire to touch her, even as her touch on his arm unsettled him. Though her job offended him, he couldn't deny that her body appealed to him on a visceral level.

"I don't know much about small towns," he drawled. "But I do know business, and I've made this town my business. You'd better get used to having me around."

~

ARIA DIDN'T LIKE men who thought they could get their way simply because they were rich and powerful—and, okay, ridiculously good-looking. They ticked her off. Her fingers curled tighter into his arm.

He spoke again, his voice no more than a rumble. "You know you're still on my property, right?"

Dropping her hand, she reeled backwards. What a beast. She'd only wanted to have a look around and get out of there. It was hardly worth kicking up such a fuss about.

"I'm leaving," she said curtly. "I shouldn't have come. I didn't realize it would upset anyone."

Elijah Lockwood shrugged one perfectly clad shoulder. "I don't like reporters. Especially nosy ones. Trouble always follows them." He pulled a card from his coat pocket and pressed it into her palm. At his touch, jitters shot up her arm. Had a spark passed between them? Static electricity? She flinched away, unwilling to analyze the moment further. "If you have any questions about my development, call this number. Get your information firsthand."

Aria nodded, then brushed past him. Elijah Lockwood, CEO of Lockwood Holdings Limited.

Pity. He was such a good-looking brute.

CHAPTER 3

*L*ater that night, Aria's friend Avery turned up on her porch. As soon as the door opened, she brushed past Aria and sat at the kitchen table, flicking her long sable hair over her shoulder and leaning her elbows on the tabletop.

"So, you met Elijah Lockwood?" she asked, watching the cursor blink on the empty document that Aria had been trying to fill with text for her follow-up article about the development. She had yet to figure out the best angle to keep her audience engaged.

"The man has an ego the size of a small country," Aria replied. "Seemed to think I was out to get him."

"That article you wrote wasn't exactly in his favor," Avery reminded her.

"Writing an article in support wouldn't have had the same reaction from the public," Aria reasoned. "Besides, I'm working on a series, so he still has a chance to have his say."

"So, you *were* trying to stir the pot. Can't blame him for being upset."

Aria groaned. "You're supposed to be on my side."

Avery grinned widely, exposing the gum she was chewing

on. "You know he's one of the country's most eligible bachelors?"

Spinning on her chair, Aria muttered, "What's the world coming to?"

"Is he as cute as they say?"

She crossed her legs and folded her arms. "I didn't notice."

Avery tapped her foot and lifted one winged eyebrow. She clearly didn't believe Aria's purported disinterest.

"All right, so he's incredibly hot," Aria admitted. "I'm not sure I'd say cute." Not when he had those full lips, that strong jaw and the drool-worthy eyes. "More like yummy. Swoonworthy." And one cool customer.

"You should have been friendlier," Avery remarked. "You'll probably see a lot of him over the next couple of weeks. It couldn't have hurt to get off on the right foot."

"It wasn't my fault," Aria insisted. "Only... I shouldn't have gone there in the first place."

"But you did, Ri. And that's okay."

Her friend was attempting to placate her, but she didn't care. She glanced at her watch. "Time to head to Davy's."

Davy's Bar and Restaurant made the best cocktails in town, and it had become a tradition for Aria and her friends to head there on a Friday night. Housed in a building dating back to the start of the 20th century, with a concrete façade, high ceilings, off-white walls and maroon furnishings, the bar was quaint—old-fashioned but tidy.

"Hey, Soph." Aria slid onto the bar stool next to their friend Sophie Delaware and smiled at Davy behind the bar. "I'll have an Irish whiskey with chocolate milk, on the rocks, please."

Davy poured her drink and passed Avery a beer, which she uncapped and swigged heavily.

"Mm, cold and wet, just the way I like it," she joked. "Cheers."

"How was your day, Soph?" Aria asked.

Sophie crinkled her nose. At five-feet-three and twenty-five years old, Sophie was the shortest and the youngest of her friends. With her freckles, slight frame and youthful face, she was often mistaken for a high school student. "Not so great. I had no sales, and a client screamed at me."

"That's rough. Sorry," Aria said.

"Ri met a cute guy," Avery said casually.

Sophie's eyes lit with interest, her work woes forgotten. "I want to know everything."

"There's nothing to tell," Aria said. Briefly, she explained the events of the afternoon and her meeting with Elijah Lockwood. "So, really," she finished, "he doesn't have a sense of humor and thinks I'm a ninny."

"I'm sure that's not true."

Sophie was too sweet. Aria knew she'd made a fool of herself. She wished she didn't care. All she needed from Elijah Lockwood was a good story, but no woman wanted to look like an idiot in front of a handsome man.

"Your Mr. Lockwood—" Avery began.

"He's not *my* Mr. Lockwood."

"Mr. Lockwood," Avery repeated with an eye roll. "What does he look like?"

Waving a hand in the air, Aria shrugged as if to ask, 'Who cares?' "Brown hair, blue eyes, quite tall."

"Like that guy over there?" Avery asked, tilting her head toward the end of the bar.

Sure enough, Elijah Lockwood was nursing a beer only a few seats away from them. His eyes met hers. Aria jolted in her seat. Stunned, she tore her eyes away. The breath trapped in her chest rattled out unevenly as she fought the instant wave of attraction. Not now. Not with this man. She didn't need to complicate matters by being attracted to him.

Sophie's jaw went slack.

"Oh, quit drooling," Aria snapped. "He's only a man."

"You said he was cute, not gobsmackingly hot," Sophie

said, loud enough to be heard across the room. Aria begged the floor to swallow her up.

~

Did trouble never cease to follow him? Here she was, sitting at the bar: the last person Eli had expected to see. Usually, he didn't have much downtime, but with all nonessential meetings cancelled, he was at a loose end. Anyway, he needed to eat sometime. He'd barely taken a seat and asked for a beer when a splash of color caught his eye. On closer inspection, he recognized the journalist, Aria Simons, the one who was intent on ruining his plans. He couldn't have asked for a better opportunity to observe her. In his business, it paid to know your enemy.

Miss Simons appeared older than he'd originally thought, perhaps mid-twenties, although she dressed like a five-year-old girl let loose in a mall. The fluffy pink jersey and purple leggings she'd worn earlier had been joined by a blue hat and a pair of knee-high green boots. The result was eye-catching. One of those sights you couldn't look away from, no matter how much you tried.

She was with friends: a tall, willowy woman with deep-set eyes wearing jeans and a scruffy alumni hoody, and a short, slight woman wearing a pencil skirt and a white blouse with sky-high stiletto heels. One of these women should help Miss Simons with her wardrobe choices.

He didn't believe Miss Simons posed any real threat to his project, but she was likely to make a nuisance of herself. Reporters always did. For as long as he could remember, the media had been interested in his family. Eli had been raised by wealthy parents who had thrived in the media spotlight and used it to publicize their advertising company. The media had its uses, but growing up with cameras around every corner had made him jaded. Despite that, it had never bothered him overly until the mess with Victoria. Now, he preferred to avoid the media whenever possible. Happily, Lockwood Holdings Limited sold itself. Because they did good work and made good money, he rarely had to interact with journalists, publicists or media moguls.

This was different. Even though he didn't want this journalist anywhere near him, the cat was out of the bag, and he needed to get her on-side. His plans would go more smoothly if she didn't fight him the whole way. He needed to play nice and make up for his earlier abruptness. Mark, his lawyer and best friend, was constantly telling him he would get things done more quickly if he turned up the charm. As far as Eli was concerned, his job was to make money, not friends, but it couldn't hurt to sweeten Miss Simons up a bit.

He gestured to the bartender. "What's that girl having?" he asked, motioning discreetly toward the journalist. "The one who looks like she took a bath in a rainbow."

The bartender grinned. "That's Aria," he said, speaking with a trace of an Irish accent. "You've got your eye on a good'un. A real sweetheart. She's having Irish whiskey tonight."

Irish whiskey from an Irish bartender. Go figure.

"Send her another one. On me."

"Want me to mention you?"

Eli shook his head and settled back again to watch the three women. After a few seconds, the taller one turned to face him. He met her gaze until she looked away. Moments later, Aria looked up at him. Her brow furrowed, and she began to say something to her friends but was interrupted by the bartender.

~

"HEY, Ri, drink for you. From the out-o'-towner." Davy interrupted Aria's thoughts, offering her a glass.

22

"He sent it?" she asked, following Davy's gaze to Elijah Lockwood. "Tell him thanks, but no thanks."

"Are you crazy?" Sophie interjected, stopping Davy before he could leave. "Hot guy sends you a drink and you send it back?"

"It's bribery," Aria said. "He wants me to write nice things about him."

"So *what*? When was the last time someone bought you a drink?" Sophie asked. "For that matter, when was the last time you slept with someone?"

"*Excuse me?*"

Sophie rolled her eyes. "Come on, Ri. When?"

"How is that relevant?"

"Why are you avoiding the question?"

Aria thought hard. She counted back eighteen months. It couldn't have been that long ago. "I don't remember," she hedged.

Sophie's expression was disbelieving. "When was the last time you even dated?"

"Well, there was Hemi..."

"That was three months ago, and you only went to the movies. Once."

Aria sighed. She could see where this was going.

"You never give anyone a chance, Aria. You don't have enough fun. Why not accept a drink from tall-dark-and-rich?"

"It would compromise my objectivity."

Avery chuckled. "You and your bloody morals. Don't send the drink back. I'll have it."

"She who only drinks beer wants the whiskey?" Sophie raised an eyebrow. "You won't appreciate it. Besides, if the hottie wants female company, it's going to be me." She ignored their disapproving expressions. "Having sex with him isn't going to compromise my morals. I won't marry the guy. He looks like he could show a girl a good time, that's all."

Sophie took the drink from Davy and sipped, her eyes meeting Elijah's over the brim. She waggled her eyebrows.

"Please, Soph," Avery groaned. "Have *some* self-respect."

Aria watched Elijah watch Sophie. She thought maybe his lips twitched up at the corners in the faintest hint of amusement. Only for a moment. Then cold detachment returned. "He's so arrogant," she muttered. *And so gorgeous.*

"So hot," Sophie sighed, echoing Aria's thoughts.

"Aren't you and Evan seeing each other at the moment?" Aria asked, poking Sophie's shoulder.

"We're having time out."

"Thank god," Avery exclaimed. "Don't go back there, Soph. That guy is scum."

Evan Wright was her on-again off-again boyfriend. He was a solicitor, and, in Aria's opinion, not good enough to lick the shoes on Sophie's feet. But there was no telling Sophie that. Wanting to hold on to their friendship, Aria tolerated Evan in the hope that her friend would come to her senses. Unfortunately, Avery wasn't as understanding, and disparaged Evan at every opportunity.

The man was handsome, in a smooth, lawyerly way, and as wealthy as they came in Itirangi. He'd also had a string of pretty secretaries who'd made cow eyes at him. And Sophie—poor, sweet Sophie—believed he'd never laid a hand on any of them. Their friend was, quite simply, deluded.

"Oh, leave it be, Avery," Aria said, receiving a dark look in return. "Let's play pool."

The others agreed, eager to smooth over the awkward moment. Aria collected the balls and cue sticks from Davy, shrugging when he winked at her—he knew she was awful at pool. Despite her best efforts, she often knocked the ball off the table or missed the shot completely. It was common knowledge that Aria had no hand-eye coordination, and while most other people would be embarrassed, she was so used to her clumsiness that it didn't really bother her anymore.

~

Elijah drank his second beer and kept an eye on Aria Simons and her friends. After the small one had accepted his drink, they'd completely dismissed him. He wasn't sure whether to be irritated or amused. Being ignored was a new experience for him, although 'ignoring' would imply a certain degree of awareness. It seemed more likely they'd forgotten his existence altogether. Eli checked the time, later than he'd thought. He really ought to head to the villa and unpack, but something kept him glued where he was.

The girls had migrated from the bar to the pool table and begun to play, recruiting one of the men who'd been watching rugby on the flat screen so they would have evenly numbered teams. After the first few turns, the tall girl and her partner had put away three balls, the small girl had put away one, and Aria had knocked the white ball off the table twice. Did she know how bad she was? She must. Good lord, it was painful watching her.

Eli was brilliant at pool. His parents had always told him that if he was going to bother doing something, he should be the best at it.

The journalist lined up another shot, purple legs stretched out as she reached across the table. Didn't she know it would work better if she walked around the table so she didn't have to reach so far? She swung back, then missed the ball. Eli couldn't take it anymore. He crossed the room and stood behind her. She shifted on her feet, trying to get into a better position.

"You're doing it wrong," he said. She jumped, whacking her knee on the edge of the table and landing on his foot. He grunted as his big toe exploded in pain.

"What the hell are you doing?" Her eyes were big, brown and accusing.

"Helping," he replied. "It'll work better this way." Gently, he turned her around and adjusted her waist so she was tucked up against him. He extended her arms and shifted the cue stick so it rested between her thumb and forefinger.

"Just be gentle," he said, swaying the cue stick back, then forwards, knocking a ball into the far-right pocket. "Like that."

Eli took a few moments to enjoy the wide-eyed expression on her face before he released her and strode out of the bar. As he pulled his jacket tighter around his shoulders, he couldn't help recalling the curve of her body, the way she'd been pressed against him so deliciously.

Forget it. You've been single for far too long.

CHAPTER 4

*T*he girls burst into laughter the moment he left the bar.

"You should see the look on your face!" Sophie exclaimed. "Priceless!"

Avery wolf-whistled. "I think it's getting hot in here."

"Oh, shut up." Aria shook her head, bemused. Who did Elijah Lockwood think he was? Normal, respectful people didn't invade someone's personal space upon the barest acquaintance. They didn't make fun of said stranger's poor pool-playing ability. And they certainly didn't make her *feel* things she had no business feeling. Hot, fluttery things.

It wasn't right.

Then again, Elijah Lockwood was stinking rich. Combine that with his decent—okay, fantastic—looks, and he probably got away with everything. That wasn't the way Aria operated. Money and power did nothing to improve her opinion of men. If anything, she was warier of powerful men. They could do more damage. She reminded herself of how she knew that first-hand. She couldn't allow herself to think about Elijah's sexy hands, so big and strong when they'd held her own. She had to ignore the flash of attraction and the thousand butterflies that had set up camp in her stomach. Nothing good could come of Mr. Lockwood and his propensity for touching her.

The last time her name had been connected with a powerful man's, she'd been tossed out of her fabulous job, scorned by her colleagues, and labelled a woman who used sexual favors for career advancement. No matter how untrue it was. After a year and two hundred kilometers of distance, she was beginning to restore her reputation and leave the bitterness behind. Now, if only she could earn this promotion, she could prove to everyone that she'd deserved it the first time around. And finally, she'd have her pride back.

"Wait until I tell Justin about this," Sophie teased, drawing Aria out of her thoughts.

"You wouldn't dare."

Justin was Aria's oldest brother. He and Cooper, her other brother, were fiercely protective. Justin, because he'd had his own heart broken, and Cooper, because he was afraid that a man like himself—a playboy of the first order—might misuse his baby sister.

Her brothers were one of the reasons Aria rarely dated. The other reason was, she couldn't bring herself to trust a man. Not yet. She hadn't slept with Wilson Jones, but his unwanted advances and the horrific consequences had tainted her view of men. Since then, she hadn't met anyone for whom it seemed worth risking her heart and braving her brothers' interference. Dating had been much easier before Wilson Jones and before she'd moved home. Everyone in Itirangi watched her so closely. They did it out of love, but it was exhausting. Aria adored her brothers. She did. But they could be a goddamn nuisance.

"Really, Soph," she said. "A man looks at me sideways, and you're ready to run to my brothers? This is how rumors start." The words came out harsh when she meant to be teasing, but she couldn't help it. Men were a touchy subject.

Sophie winced, avoiding eye contact in the way Aria had become used to when someone was uncomfortable around her.

"Calm down, Ri," Avery said. "Sophie didn't mean it that way."

Sophie nodded, obviously hurt. "You know I think you should get back on the horse. I'd never start a rumor or mess with your love life."

"Sorry, Soph." Aria already felt silly for overreacting. "You hit a nerve, I guess."

"I guess so." Sophie's forehead creased down the middle. "I should have thought before I spoke."

"It's not your fault." Aria looked away and picked up the pool cue, ready to pretend that Elijah Lockwood had never entered the bar and this conversation had never happened. After a moment, her friends followed suit. The man they'd asked to join them was long gone. Aria didn't blame him.

Each Saturday, Aria liked to spend a couple of hours coming up with ideas for articles she could write the following Sunday, to be published in Monday's paper. This Saturday was no exception. The application Elijah Lockwood had submitted to the council for a permit to construct his shopping complex and motel made fascinating Saturday-night reading. On Sunday morning, she wrote an article outlining the main details of the project and created a side-by-side comparison of the current site and the concept plan drawn up by the architect.

It would be a beautiful building, made of creamy stone with big windows, but it wasn't right for Itirangi. Too modern. Too big. Too sophisticated. Their town was a back-water, and that was part of its appeal. Time moved more slowly. People floated across the lake in kayaks and dinghies

—no power boats allowed—or they read books on the lake shore during the summer.

In the winter, snow bleached the hills and mountains, and when the ski season began, everyone wrapped up in jackets and scarves. The snow on the lakeside sparkled, and sometimes, young brides posed for photos, certain that the pristine white backdrop contrasting with the deep blue lake would elevate their wedding day from special to magnificent.

Aria's research revealed that Mr. Lockwood had somehow managed to acquire an old villa near the center of town, quite a feat in the midst of tourist season. No doubt one of the perks of being obscenely wealthy.

On Monday morning at 9 a.m., she visited the villa to interview him. From the outside, the place was run down, with paint peeling off the weather-boards and lichen growing on the roof. None of the windows had curtains, so the morning light silhouetted objects inside. The garden was growing wild, and ivy covered one outside wall. She wondered idly if the poor state of the house was the reason he'd been able to get access to it on such short notice. Usually, accommodation in Itirangi was booked months in advance, and each time a house came up for sale, a bidding war ensued.

As she hesitated on the doorstep, she shivered from the unseasonal chill in the air. Two minutes passed, and no one answered her knock, so she decided to try the door handle. It was unlocked. Should she go in? If she did, would she regret it later? Probably. Did she care? No. She *needed* this story. She wasn't afraid to tiptoe along the boundary of right and wrong to achieve it.

After another moment of hesitation, she pushed the door open and stepped inside, into a high-ceilinged hallway with surprisingly thick red carpet. It smelled musty. The walls were bare save for faded floral wallpaper, and the house was eerily silent. It felt like the setting of a bad horror film, the sort with bucketloads of fake blood and corpses falling from the ceiling. She shoved her hands into her armpits, arms hugging her chest as she walked forwards. The door swung shut, closing her in.

"Hello," she called out, reluctant to go any farther from the exit. "Is anyone home?"

Hearing nothing, she tiptoed down the hall, passing at least half a dozen closed doors. She imagined cavernous bedchambers with canopied beds and fireplaces set into the walls. At the end of the hall, a door was slightly ajar. Pushing it open, she peered into the darkness. When her eyes adjusted, she could see a coffee table and an enormous couch in the center of the room. A bundle of newspaper with a few greasy chips lay on the coffee table.

A soft rustle startled her, and she shrieked, her hand leaping to cover her racing heart.

"What the hell?"

Too late, Aria realized a person was sleeping on the couch. Or rather, a person had been sleeping on the couch. A large body rose from it, outlined by the light filtering through the murky glass. She backed away quickly and considered running for the exit. Coming here had been a very bad idea. Coming inside had been an even worse one, the kind of thing that got her into trouble on a regular basis. Her brothers were always telling her she had no sense, and she was beginning to believe it.

"Stop." The voice was so commanding, she felt it right down to her toes, and they became glued to the ground. "What are you doing here?"

One mystery solved. Now that he was upright, she could confirm that the man on the couch was indeed Elijah Lockwood. Unfortunately, he didn't seem pleased to see her.

"Um... I'm..." Aria floundered, disconcerted at being alone with him in a dark room. The situation was both awkward and alarmingly intimate. "Is it all right if I turn on the light?"

31

"Please do."

Aria ran her fingers along the wall, found the switch and flicked the lights on, then blinked until her eyes readjusted. She was not prepared for the sight that greeted her. Elijah Lockwood, CEO of Lockwood Holdings Limited, stood before her wearing blue flannel pajamas, his tousled hair hanging over his forehead. Despite his pajamas, he managed to look quite forbidding. If Aria had been sensible, or even had some instincts of self-preservation, she would have apologized and excused herself. But she'd never been accused of being sensible. So, instead, she burst out laughing.

"What's so funny?" he demanded, advancing until only a foot of air separated them. At another time, she might have found it intimidating. Now, not so much. "You've barged into my house at some ridiculous hour of the morning. You'd better have a good reason for it."

Aria wished she could take him seriously—really, she did —but it was impossible. Eventually, she forced herself to stop laughing and take a few deep breaths. Then, once the hilarity had faded, she was struck by a different thought. Elijah filled out those pajamas very well. And he was so close. She hadn't taken much notice when he pressed up against her on Friday night, but his wide shoulders tapered down to a narrow waist and muscular thighs. The top two buttons of the pajamas were undone, exposing a light dusting of hair across his chest. She gulped and fought the desire to run her hands up his body to see whether it was as firm as it looked.

Not appropriate, Ri!

"I'm sorry," she muttered. "I didn't know you'd be asleep. Most people would be up by now."

"It doesn't pay to make assumptions," he rumbled, rubbing the sleep out of his eyes.

The movement lifted the bottom of his top, giving her a glimpse of his stomach. Aria's mouth watered. If only he would stretch a little more, so she could tell if his torso was as toned as she suspected.

"Miss Simons."

Aria tore her gaze away from the exposed skin and saw his knowing smile. Too smug. He knew exactly where she'd been looking, blast it all.

"Why are you here?"

His expression held a hint of interest. Was it possible she affected him in the same way he affected her? She studied his face for symptoms of attraction. Nope. Nothing. Nada.

"Miss Simons." Frustration laced his voice, but she thought she detected a flicker of amusement in his icy eyes, a slight softening of the lines around his mouth.

"Aria," she said. She hated being called Miss Simons. It made her feel like a school teacher.

"Aria," he corrected himself. "You should know my sense of humor isn't the best in the morning. Tell me why you're here, or I'll have to pick you up and throw you out."

Determined not to be cowed, and also not to think about what it would feel like to have his arms around her body, she said, "I was hoping to interview you about your development."

"You couldn't ring and make an appointment? I did give you my number."

This had to be the strangest conversation she'd ever had. "You did," she said. "But I prefer to be spontaneous. So, how about it? I'm here anyway."

"Now?" He said it as if she'd requested he strip naked and dance in front of the queen. Not that she'd object to seeing that, mind you.

"That *is* why I'm here," she reminded him.

He snorted and massaged his temples. "You're not going to go away, are you?"

"Nope," she said cheerfully. "You wanted a chance to tell me your point of view. This is it."

"Miss Simons—"

"Aria."

"Aria." He crossed his arms. "I don't want to give you another story. I want you to retract your previous story and leave me the hell alone. Believe it or not, I don't exist solely as fodder for newspapers and magazines."

She rolled her eyes. "I've already told you I'm not retracting my story. I'm not ashamed of it, and I won't let you bully me. Now, about that interview."

"Give it up!" His exasperation was evident in the way he ran a hand roughly through his hair, tugging at the ends. "I don't know if you've noticed, but I'm in my pajamas."

"Oh, I noticed," she replied, smiling cheekily. "They're adorable. Not quite what I'd pictured, but still—"

"They're my pajamas! You broke into the house, woke me before I was ready, and you expect me to string together coherent sentences? Give me a moment to catch up, woman. And for god's sake, give me a chance to get dressed."

This wasn't going the way Aria had imagined. She wasn't sure whether to press her advantage while he was off his game or bow out gracefully. Clearly, he required more patience than she'd anticipated, but she resolved to put him in a better mood so she could get the most out of him.

"How about I make breakfast while you have a shower?" she suggested. Everyone felt better after a refreshing shower in the morning. Even cranky businessmen.

Elijah sighed and ran that hand through his hair again. "Fine," he agreed. "Give me ten minutes."

CHAPTER 5

$\mathcal{E}$li took his time in the shower, both cooling his temper and hoping Aria would discover the empty cupboards, get bored and leave. She seemed the type to get distracted easily. But luck was not on his side. The smell of recently cooked food wafted through the house, and his mouth watered as he neared the kitchen. When he passed through the lounge, he noted his rubbish had been cleared away and the coffee table wiped down. As he entered the kitchen, he couldn't help but grin at the enormous omelet and the cup of coffee waiting on the dining table. She was resourceful; he'd give her that. Sitting on the opposite side of the four-person table, she was sipping a bright pink drink.

"Where did this come from?" he asked. "I haven't done any shopping. The cupboards were empty."

"I know. You were taking a while in the shower, so I whipped down to the bakehouse."

That explained it. He was oddly pleased that she hadn't tried to convince him she'd magicked food out of nothing. Other women might have done so to impress him.

She looked good this morning. He hadn't paid attention

earlier, but she was fresh-faced and bright-eyed, with ringlets of brown hair cascading down her back from a braid that ended at the nape of her neck. She was wearing a high-waisted Hawaiian-print dress which drew attention to her well-endowed upper half. Eli's gaze lingered on the swell of her breasts; they would be more than a handful for the average person, but he had large hands and itched to see how they fit. The soft edge of her skirt brushed against thighs that were golden and shapely.

Eye contact. Make eye contact.

It wouldn't do to let her catch him admiring her—even if she had made love to him with her eyes earlier. The way she'd nibbled her lip as her eyes focused on his bare skin had been downright sexy, and also completely unintentional, based on the way she'd blushed when he said her name. She was a woman who seemed unaware of her allure. Refreshing. She was worrying the pink lipstick off with her teeth, and his lower half sprang to attention. Hurriedly, he slid onto the chair before she could notice. Although he didn't like having his house invaded, he appreciated that she was here to listen to his plans, which was all the more surprising because of how he'd manhandled her on Friday.

"Thanks," he grunted as he dug into the omelet, grateful for the distraction.

She opened a paper bag and drew out a slice of chocolate cake. Taking a bite, she hummed in pleasure. Abruptly, his appetite for food disappeared, and he was hungry for something else.

"You have cake for breakfast?" he asked, trying to sound disapproving rather than turned on.

"Mm." A fleck of chocolate caught on her lip, and she licked it off. "Sometimes. I'm vegetarian, so there aren't many savory options for me at the bakery. This was the best they had." She paused for a moment, then added guiltily, "Well, it wasn't the best option, but it was the yummiest. I have a huge sweet tooth."

Despite himself, Eli was intrigued. What sort of adult ate dessert for breakfast? He felt control of the situation slipping from his grasp and sought desperately for a way to get it back. Business. They could discuss business. He had a cool head and was widely respected as an up-and-coming entrepreneurial powerhouse. He could handle this. After all, he was an expert at shutting down dangerous situations before they exploded.

"What questions do you have?" he asked.

If Aria was surprised by the change of topic, she did nothing to show it. "I've got a few about your mall. Your company. Your personal life. I thought I'd write a profile outlining who you are, what you do, and your aims for this development."

"Is 'no comment' an acceptable answer?" Some things, personal things, he didn't want to share. He'd had his private life splashed across a tabloid magazine before and had no desire for a repeat.

Her teeth latched onto her full bottom lip. "If you're not comfortable with a question, you can refuse to answer."

"You won't misrepresent my opinion or take it out of context?"

"Mr. Lockwood." She sounded indignant.

"Eli," the devil drove him to say.

"What?" A furrow formed between her brows.

"If I can call you Aria, then you should call me Eli. It's only fair."

"Okay," she drawled. "Eli it is. Now, Eli, whatever your opinion of journalism is as a whole, I have a set of professional ethics. I don't twist facts. If I have only one set of facts, then my article may seem unbalanced. That's the way it is. But I never write or imply anything that's untrue." She hesitated. "I may be guilty of blowing things out of proportion from time to time. It's a hazard of the job."

Her tone was sincere, her eyes clear and her expression encouraging. Oddly enough, he believed her. Her final comment caused him some concern, though. "What's your first question?"

Before he had time to reconsider, she'd dug her notebook out of her handbag. "An easy one to begin with," she said. "Why Itirangi?"

He frowned while he considered the question. "I've already built complexes in every city in the country, but I'm not ready to stop. I want to take my company further. Itirangi is fast becoming a popular tourist destination, but no one else seems willing to take a chance on it yet. I've studied every possible scenario, and it's a good investment. I'm ahead of the ball game."

～

Jotting down the important parts of his reply, Aria got the feeling there was more behind his project than numbers. "You really believe in your work here, don't you?"

"I think it will be good for my company and for the town," he answered.

"Have you considered how it will affect the local businesses, which have been doing pretty well from the tourist market up until now?"

He shrugged and sipped his coffee. "More amenities in the area can only be good for them, since they'll draw more tourists in."

It surprised Aria that he'd even considered the matter, let alone formulated an opinion on it. He *had* read her article last week. Surely, in the face of that, some hesitancy was to be expected? But then, she supposed businessmen didn't make millions by doing things half-heartedly. She dug her nails into her palms to stop herself from lecturing him about the good of the town, which she knew far more about than he did. Instead, she referred to her list of questions.

"What are your favorite and least favorite parts of the job?"

"My favorite part is the beginning," he replied immediately. "Finding a new location, scouting out the competition, coming up with a plan of attack. My least favorite part is the human factor."

His response intrigued her. "The human factor?"

"You may not have noticed, but I have little patience for dealing with people."

His tone was self-deprecating, and she liked him more for it. It was nice to know he was aware of his flaws. It was also good for her article. She could picture it already: 'Antisocial businessman cares little for people.' If she could convince herself to expose him to a public flaying of his reputation. Unlikely.

He continued. "Employees, designers, architects, media liaison staff... They're there to talk to the right people and make things happen. I'd rather make sure the other details are taken care of."

"Is that what you do? Sort out the details?"

"I do manage people to a certain degree," he admitted. "It may surprise you, but I'm not good at delegation."

"You're a control freak," she said, chuckling. "You don't know how to loosen your grip on the reins."

He wasn't amused. "Next question."

"When are you expecting your work here to be completed?"

"July. From the beginning of construction, it's a six-month project."

"When did you start your company, and why?"

"Are the rest of your questions all this personal? Shouldn't we focus on the development?"

He thought this was personal? Aria scanned over the other questions on her list and crossed a couple off. No need to give the poor man an aneurysm. "This is a profile of you and your company," she reminded him. "It's a small town. People are fascinated by outsiders."

"Right." He gazed around the room, at everything but her. "I started the company nine years ago, when I was fresh out of university. My parents wanted me to join their advertising firm, but it didn't appeal to me. I wanted to push myself to succeed without their help."

"I think you've done that admirably," she said. "They must be proud."

Eli scoffed. "Off the record, they're bitterly disappointed that I didn't put my management skills to better use in the family business."

"That's not fair," she protested. "I'm sure they're proud of you, no matter what career path you've taken."

His face was a study in disbelief.

She swallowed. Apparently not. "What did you study at university?"

"Easy." He looked disappointed. "Business and project management."

"Do you have any siblings?"

"A sister."

"Name?"

"Therese."

"How old?"

"Fifteen."

Interesting. "She's much younger than you. Is there a reason for that?"

"My parents forgot contraception, I guess."

It was like getting blood from a stone. Endlessly frustrating. "You don't say very much, do you?"

He grinned, and the effect softened his features, making

him insanely attractive. Aria's stomach buzzed with something that wasn't nerves.

"I prefer to speak only if I have something to say," he told her.

"The strong, silent type, huh?" she teased, a smile flirting with the corners of her lips.

"Not exactly."

She leaned toward him. "What an interesting statement. You realize you're playing into the stereotype, right?"

He smiled again but didn't say anything. The flutters quadrupled. Clearing her throat, she ignored them and checked her list. Only a couple of questions left.

"Is there a Mrs. Lockwood?" The question came out high-pitched and breathless. Squeezing her eyes shut, she willed herself to sound normal. "Or another Mr. Lockwood, perhaps?"

"No. To both," he clarified. "I don't have a wife, girlfriend or significant other." He raked his gaze over her from head to toes, blue eyes blazing. "But I enjoy female company. For the record."

"Oh," she breathed, pinned down by the heat in his eyes. "I see."

"Do you?" Now he leaned forward, making her feel caged in, even with the table between them.

"You're single," she squeaked, then coughed, trying to recover her voice. "And you like women."

"'Like' is such a bland word." He radiated heat. Though he hadn't moved, she could feel the warmth caressing her skin. "I *desire* intelligent, curvy, maddening women who ask too many questions."

His statement had come entirely from left field, and it agitated the butterflies taking up residence in her belly. Not to mention, his statement was dangerous. No matter how he made her feel, or perhaps *because* of how he made her feel, Eli was dangerous to her reputation and her hard-earned self-respect.

She shot to her feet, clutching the notepad to her chest. "I've got enough for the article," she said quickly. "Thanks for the interview. I'll let myself out."

Then she was out the door, in her car and heading to the office, leaving Elijah Lockwood at the kitchen table, smug as a cat with the cream.

The bastard.

CHAPTER 6

*H*e shouldn't have said it. He really shouldn't have. But, damn it, with her looking so fresh and pretty, asking him about the state of his love life, Eli couldn't resist. He shouldn't have provoked her, but it had certainly been worth it, especially when interest had sparked in her eyes before she'd fled from the house. Aria wasn't as immune to him as she pretended to be. And, shit, he wasn't immune to her either. He just crossed his fingers that teasing her didn't come back to bite him in the ass, either in private or in a newspaper headline. For a few minutes there, he'd forgotten the power she wielded as a member of the press.

Eli shook his head, dispelling all thoughts of the sexy journalist. He had a lot of things to do today; he couldn't afford to waste time fantasizing about her or worrying what she might do with the information he'd given her. Since he'd decided to stay in Itirangi to see this project out, he'd had to make arrangements for Therese, who was staying with him for the last month of summer. She'd be arriving later in the day to join him, and he needed to prepare a bedroom for her. Being a multimillionaire, he'd thought he was above menial chores like cleaning and airing out a rambling villa; however, in his haste to get to Itirangi, he hadn't brought any staff with him. But he could manage to look after himself for a few months. Surely.

Therese would no doubt interfere with the work he had planned, but her coming here couldn't be avoided. Their parents had already arranged to fly her down. Frances, his mother, would drop her off on her way to a business meeting in Dunedin.

He'd seen very little of Therese over the last ten years. They were strangers to each other, but, apparently, she'd become unruly and difficult for his parents to handle. They hoped spending time with Eli would improve her, which amused him since he was such a disappointment to them. Everyone knew they were grooming Therese to take over the family business. The fact that they had sunk low enough to ask him for help was telling. The situation must be dire.

BY THE TIME Therese and Frances arrived, Eli had vacuumed the entire house, removed the cobwebs and installed curtains. He'd flung the doors wide open so the place could air out, and set up a laptop in a room designated as his office.

The gravel in the driveway crunched, heralding their arrival. Right on time, as usual. Frances was always punctual. Walking to the door as slowly as possible, wanting to postpone the inevitable, he wondered again how he'd ended up in this situation. Reluctant mentor to a troubled girl. Teenage girls were a foreign species. Neither he nor Therese could possibly benefit from this arrangement. Unfortunately, it was a done deal. Frances had out-maneuvered him at every turn. Sighing, he shoved the door open and paced down the stairs. She was already unloading bags from the boot of a late model Ford Falcon—classy and practical, like her.

"Hi, Mother." Eli greeted her with a cool smile that didn't

reach his eyes. His family weren't affectionate. They hadn't been raised that way.

"Elijah," she acknowledged, patting her stylish auburn bob, although not a hair was out of place. Her hazel eyes held a hint of condescension as she scanned him from head to toe. "Therese refuses to leave the car," she told him, flicking a piece of lint from the shoulder of her navy-blue power suit. "I don't know where she learned to be so mule-headed."

"It's a mystery, Mother." Eli found it best to neither agree nor disagree with anything she said. Being stubbornly neutral was the least painful way to get through meetings with her.

He tapped on the car window and was struck speechless. His mouth gaped, and his brain emptied. Who was this girl? She certainly wasn't the sister he remembered, a wholesome girl with strawberry blonde curls and chubby cheeks. No, the girl facing him had bleached hair that haphazardly fell over her face as she jerked her chin up and glared at him. The little curls that used to enchant him were gone, straightened into submission. Pale makeup caked her face and dark eyeliner ringed her eyes, making her look ghoulish. She stepped out of the car, and he noticed that the denim shorts she was wearing revealed the bottom of her underwear.

"What happened?" he blurted out. Her eyes narrowed. Shit, he should have been more diplomatic. "You look different."

"You look exactly the same," she replied, making it sound like an insult. Hands on her hips, she leaned back and scowled at the villa. "*This* is my prison for the next month?"

"It could do with a bit of fixing up," he admitted.

"It could do with a wrecking ball and a stick of dynamite."

Eli was too startled to reply. What had happened to that sweet, freckly-faced kid?

"Be grateful she's talking at all," Frances said. "She doesn't say much these days."

She finished retrieving bags and closed the boot, then headed back to the driver's door.

"Aren't you going to come in?" he asked.

"Business calls." The words were abrupt. "I'm right on schedule, as long as I keep moving."

"Of course." Why was he surprised? He shouldn't have expected anything else. Never mind that he hadn't seen either of his parents for six months. It shouldn't bother him, yet it did. If he had kids, he would make sure to keep in touch even when they were older. At least he thought he would. But it was a moot point, because he never planned to be a father. He hadn't had a pleasant childhood, and he wouldn't subject any child to the same. Business came first. He knew his priorities.

When she offered it, Eli shook his mother's hand, but Therese pretended not to notice when Frances turned to her.

"Mothers don't shake hands," she said. "They hug. You're a robot imposter."

"Mind yourself, darling," Frances cautioned.

Therese maintained a stony silence as their mother slid into the front seat, wound up the window and pulled out of the drive.

"I'll show you your room," Eli said awkwardly, collecting her bags from the ground. "I hope you'll like it. We can change a few things if you want to." When she didn't reply, he tried again. "Did you have a good trip?"

She rolled her blue eyes and stalked up the steps, leaving Eli to carry the bags. "Which room?"

"Second door on the left."

She yanked the door open and sighed. The room met with her disapproval, as did the kitchen, the lounge, the bathroom, and the back yard. The house was 'stuffy', 'ancient', and 'smells like someone died in it'. The criticisms kept flowing in. Then, once she'd let her general displeasure be known, she was silent.

46

Perhaps, if she continued to be quiet, the next month would be more peaceful than he'd thought. One could hope.

~

"Your articles aren't what I expected," Eliza Brown said as she joined Aria on a lakeside bench.

Aria nodded. "I know. I'm building up to something. I just..." *Haven't worked up the courage to publicly denounce Eli yet.* "I'm straightening out a few facts first." She shrugged, gazing out over the water. It was turbulent today, more grey than blue, and waves rippled against the shore—a sign of bad weather in the mountains. "I've written about the concerns of local business owners, and I've written his perspective. I just need to figure out what comes next."

"There's a storm coming," Eliza said, watching the water. Aria wasn't sure if she was referring to the weather. "Do you know what angle you'll take next?"

"I've got a couple of ideas," Aria replied, shivering as a cool breeze stirred the air. "I'm hoping to interview a couple of councilors to get their perspectives. Maybe write a profile on one of the locals who will be affected. Get a human-interest story."

Eliza lifted her chin. "Choose your councilors carefully. And your interviewee."

"With all due respect, Eliza, I always do."

"You should run another article along with it," Eliza said. "Look into Mr. Lockwood's personal background. Every well-off man has skeletons in the closet."

Aria resisted the idea, even though she knew Eliza was speaking sense. She needed a sensational story, and scandals involving handsome, successful men always rocked the boat. She knew this personally, and it was on that personal level that the thought of spreading gossip revolted her.

Aria rose to her feet to dispose of her hot chocolate cup

in the bin at the end of the bench. "I'm not a gossip columnist. I don't write that sort of news. It ruins people's lives, and I won't take part in it. I'd expect you to know that."

The older woman sighed. "I do, Miss Simons. But it never hurts to try. I don't suppose you'd be open to flirting with him?"

Aria chuckled, dismissing the idea instantly. It was a ludicrous suggestion, and she preferred not to take it seriously. Although Eli Lockwood appealed to her on many levels, she couldn't give in to the attraction. He was too powerful. There were too many ways it could go wrong.

"Nice try," she said. "But I doubt Mr. Lockwood's mind can be changed by a little flirtation. He's a rich, good-looking man from the city. I doubt he has any problems with women. What would he want with little old me?"

"Word is, he bought you a drink the other night."

All of a sudden, Aria felt sick. If rumors were spreading already, then it would only be a matter of time before they were blown out of proportion.

"He did," Aria said. "I didn't accept it."

"Silly girl," Eliza murmured.

"That's your opinion." Nodding to the other woman, Aria slung her bag over her shoulder. "I'll see you later." Then she began the trek across the lake front, back to her car.

CHAPTER 7

*O*n Tuesday nights, Aria volunteered at the local animal shelter, Hayley's Haven. She'd started as a volunteer when she was fourteen, and a couple of years later, they'd offered her paid work. Working there had paid for her first car, first guitar and first date. The guitar had never been played and the date was over in fifteen minutes, but the car lasted for five years, so she considered it a good deal. Since she'd returned to town, she'd resumed her volunteer work.

This week, it was Hayley's birthday, so she planned to drop by Pretty Things, the florist and gift shop Emily owned, to pick up a gift on the way. She was across the road when a police car cruised past and stopped right outside Pretty Things. Wondering what on earth was happening, Aria checked both ways and hurried across the road. Sergeant Gareth Wayland got out of his car wearing a familiar expression. It said *Don't mess with me* and was his go-to tool to intimidate lawbreakers.

Aria followed him into the shop, which was oddly quiet. Usually, Emily was bustling around, humming to herself and arranging flowers in complex ways no one else would dream of. Instead, she was standing behind the counter while a teenage girl hovered in the corner, tapping her foot anxiously. Emily's hands were fisted at her sides and her eyebrows were drawn tightly together. The girl was perhaps fifteen or sixteen and blonde in that unnaturally white way. She wasn't familiar. A tourist, perhaps—Aria knew most of the local kids. The girl seemed caught between fear and defiance. Although she was pouting and sneering as if she didn't care about the trouble she was in, every so often her dark-ringed eyes stared at her toes and gave her away.

"What's going on?" Aria asked. "Gareth?"

The sergeant, a handsome man standing several inches over six feet tall, crossed his arms and glared at the girl in the corner. His strong jaw moved as he chewed on gum—a habit he'd picked up when he quit smoking. He scratched his head, ruffling caramel-colored hair. She would have found him attractive if years of friendship hadn't made her immune.

"Emily caught this young lady shoplifting," Gareth replied.

No wonder poor Emily looked overwrought. The nicest woman in town, she wasn't equipped to deal with dishonesty.

Ever curious, Aria persisted, "What was she trying to steal?"

Emily gestured towards a palm-sized wreath of daisies. Aria almost laughed, but she knew it was a serious matter. Itirangi didn't take kindly to troublemakers.

"What're you going to do about it?" she asked.

"I don't want to press charges," Emily replied. "But I thought a chat with the sergeant might be a good idea."

"You were right to call me, Em," Gareth said. He turned to the girl. "You'd better come with me."

Aria laid a hand on Gareth's shoulder and tried to smile encouragingly at the girl. "Hold on a moment. What's your name, honey?"

"Teri," the girl said, jutting her chin out. "What's yours?"

"I'm Aria." She watched the nervous up-and-down movement of the girl's foot. "Things might be easier for you if you explain why you did it."

Teri didn't reply.

The sergeant pulled away from Aria. "You want me to take her to the station for a while, Em?"

Emily looked undecided.

"Why don't you give her a warning and talk to her parents?" Aria suggested. Gareth could be frightening when he wanted to be, but no matter how intimidating he was, she'd bet that Teri was more scared of her parents. Most kids were.

Emily sighed. "Okay. But if she gets into any more trouble, it's on you, Ri."

Aria hoped she wasn't being a sucker. "What's your parents' number?" she asked, pulling her cell phone from her pocket.

"Don't bother," Teri said. "They don't care."

"I'm sure that's not true."

Gareth said something to Emily and moved on. There was a certain danger in being Emily. As the sweetest, prettiest single girl in Itirangi, all the alpha males wanted to date her. Since she wouldn't say yes to any of them, they had to settle for being overly protective from a distance. Being in her shoes would drive Aria nuts.

"It is," Teri said emphatically. "They're not from around here, anyway."

"Where are they, then?" she asked, deciding to play along with the girl's game for a while. She clearly had something to say, and Aria was willing to listen.

"Dad's in Auckland, Mum's in Dunedin. At least Dad says he's in Auckland, when really he's screwing his girlfriend in Wellington."

She was aiming to provoke a response. Aria sensed that and deliberately didn't react. "So, who can we call?"

51

"My brother." A long-suffering sigh followed the words, then a theatrical eyeroll. "I'm only stuck in this hellhole because he's here on business, and my parents can't handle me. I'm the stuff-up. He's the golden boy. They're hoping he'll rub off on me."

"What's his number?" Aria asked.

"Can you handle this?" Emily broke in.

"Yeah, sure," Aria assured her.

"I'll finish tidying up, then." Emily busied herself picking up flower trimmings. Aria suspected she didn't want to be part of any impending confrontation or unpleasantness.

Teri examined her fingernails, which Aria noticed were short and ragged.

"Your brother's number?" she repeated.

Teri sighed again, dragging it out painfully. "Oh-two-seven-two-six-four-one-eight-nine-six."

Aria dialed, and a terse voice greeted her. "Lockwood."

"Mr. Lockwood?" she tested, startled to hear his voice on the other end of the phone. "It's Aria Simons here."

"Aria. To what do I owe the pleasure?" His deep voice sent shivers racing up her spine, as did the memory of his last words to her: *I desire intelligent, curvy, maddening women.*

"I've got your sister here," she said.

Silence on the other end. Then: "Therese?"

"I assume so," she answered. "Blonde. Doesn't talk much."

"That's her." Elijah's voice was weary, and she couldn't help but feel sorry for him. She doubted he had the faintest clue as to how to take care of a troublesome younger sister.

"We're at Pretty Things," Aria told him. "The local florist. Do you know how to find it?"

He didn't, so she gave him a few directions and said to be quick. "What's this about?" he asked before ending the call.

"I'll explain when you get here," she said. "I'm sorry to drag you away from work."

"It's not your fault," he muttered. "I'll be there soon."

The phone went dead, and Aria met Teri's eyes. "I wouldn't want to be you when he gets here," she said. "He sounded annoyed."

Teri stayed silent. It seemed to be her favorite method of communication.

"So, Eli is your brother? The golden boy?" She recalled the bitter twist to his mouth when he was talking about his parents during her interview. The silly man thought they were disappointed in him. Did he not realize they would never entrust their impressionable young daughter to him unless they thought he'd be a good influence? But then, such a logical thought wouldn't have crossed his stubborn male mind.

"Yes," Teri replied, scuffing the toe of her shoe on the floor. "What's it to you?"

Aria ignored the question. "He's supposed to be a good example for you, huh? Put you on the straight and narrow."

"Yeah, I guess so."

"That's a lot of pressure on him, isn't it?"

Teri looked up, eyes wide with surprise. "I hadn't thought of it that way."

"Maybe you could give him a break." Aria got the feeling Eli wasn't given many breaks.

Teri shrugged, but she was thinking about it. "You know my brother?"

Aria wrinkled her nose. "We've met."

Teri laughed, and it brightened her whole face; she'd be very pretty if she didn't try so hard to look cool. It was tough at that age, though. Aria had never had a chance to be cool because she'd been shy and chubby. She'd rallied at university, where she'd found her self-confidence and her own unique style. She'd realized she didn't have to be the prettiest girl in the room if she could be the most interesting.

"I don't really know Eli," she said. "I'm a reporter. I've interviewed him about his project here."

"Oh." There was a wealth of meaning in the word.

"What?" Aria asked, baffled.

"Eli hates reporters," Teri explained. "He always has, but especially after what happened with his ex. He thinks I don't remember, but it wasn't that long ago, and it was kind of a big deal."

What happened with his ex? Aria filed the question away as something to investigate in future. For some reason, the thought of him with another woman annoyed her. Not that it made any sense, but he'd looked at her with fire in his eyes. She liked to think he wouldn't look at her like that if he was hung up on someone else. But perhaps he was a flirt.

"Mum and Dad are business nuts, like Eli," Teri continued, oblivious to the fact that she'd piqued Aria's curiosity with the comment about her brother. "They're disappointed in me because I don't care about the business."

Aria did her best to follow the conversation. "Surely, having your brother in business is enough? Can't you do something else?"

Teri scoffed. "As if. No way. It's the business or, like, total abandonment. There's no other choice. Eli didn't take over the company, so now I have to, but I don't even know if I want it."

"So, tell them that."

"You don't think I have?"

Aria was silent. She could understand wanting your parents to be proud of you. A change of subject was in order.

A light above the door flashed red. Talk about being saved by the bell. Big brother Eli had arrived.

CHAPTER 8

Smoke ought to be pouring from his ears. The phone call he'd received hadn't shed any light on the matter, but Eli was good at reading between the lines. Therese had done something wrong. He knew this because Aria had been reluctant to speak to him, and she didn't seem like a shrinking violet. Of course, her hesitancy could be attributed to any number of things—like the way he'd hit on her during their interview, or the ugly picture Therese had painted of him.

Eli identified Pretty Things easily by the pastel pink sign on the roadside. Situated on the main street of Itirangi, near the town square, the shop was pleasing to the eye. Inside, colorful blooms spilled from pots and stands, and a variety of quirky ornaments lay scattered around. A rack on the counter displayed handmade jewelry. Aria was standing just inside the door, and Therese was sulking in the corner like a naughty toddler. Behind the counter, a redhead was scribbling in the account book.

Eli brushed past Aria, glared at Therese, and snapped, "What have you done?"

"She tried to steal a flower arrangement," Aria said when Therese didn't respond.

Eli levelled a stare at her. She probably blamed him for bringing a delinquent into their town, and he was in no mood to be reprimanded.

"I asked Therese," he growled. "Not you. I expect her to answer for herself."

"The poor girl is probably too scared to answer," Aria said mildly.

"She committed a crime and needs to face the consequences," he replied. "It doesn't matter if she likes it or not."

"The sergeant has already talked to her," Aria told him. "She doesn't need to be yelled at. She needs a fitting punishment. I think a week without wi-fi would be appropriate."

Therese's face blanched, and she protested. Both Eli and Aria shushed her.

"If I wanted your advice, I would have asked," he said. Then, "You called the police?"

"I did," the redhead behind the counter said. "I'm Emily Parker. This is my shop."

"I apologize for the trouble," Eli said, meaning it wholeheartedly. "I'll reimburse you for any damages."

"That's not necessary," the redhead replied, her smile warming a fraction. "But I'd appreciate it if you kept her away from now on."

"I'll do my best," he promised. "But she has a mind of her own. Did you press charges?" The last thing he needed was to send Therese home with a criminal record. She was his parents' best hope to keep the business in the family. She needed a spotless record.

"No," she replied.

Eli was flooded with relief. Finally, some good news. "Oh, thank god."

"Emily caught Teri, so there's no harm done," Aria said. "But if she steals anything else, it'll be my fault for encouraging Emily to send the sergeant away. Can you keep a closer eye on her?"

Eli's relief was now tempered by wariness. He didn't want to be indebted to anyone, especially not this woman. Something about her—the way she looked, the way she spoke—got under his skin. She was attractive and unusual, but it was more than that. She made him uneasy. Perhaps he was waiting for her to pull the mat out from under him. Journalists always did.

"No one asked you to do that," he murmured. "But thank you. Like I said, I'll do my best to keep her under control."

The timer on his phone pinged, and Eli groaned. The pizza he'd put in the oven would be burnt to a crisp by the time they got back. Was anything going to go right today?

"Know any good takeaway places?" he asked.

"Punjab Palace, the Indian restaurant on the main street," Aria told him. "They make a mean curry."

"That sounds great." It really did. After a long, hard day, sitting down with a bowl of lamb vindaloo sounded like heaven.

He ordered Therese to get in the car, only now realizing she'd escaped the situation without saying a word. He stepped outside, and Aria followed him, waving to the florist. He took the chance to have a good look at her. The bright colors were gone, and instead, she was wearing a pair of track pants and a hoody. Her hair was held in a ponytail at the nape of her neck, but escaping tendrils had formed a fluffy halo. She looked normal, but no less sexy for it.

"Thank you," he said. "For helping Therese. I know you had no reason to, and I appreciate it."

Aria smiled, and her eyes lit up. In the dim light, flecks of green danced around in the irises. The woman was magical.

"You're welcome. I was glad to help."

He couldn't help but wonder at what price.

AFTER ELI LEFT, Aria released the breath she'd been holding. He was a big man, and she'd felt crowded by him. During those last few minutes, when they'd been alone, he'd positively overwhelmed her. It wasn't all because of his size, though. He possessed an animal magnetism that, she was convinced, would exert a gravitational pull on any straight female, single or not.

She bought a bouquet of sunflowers for Hayley, and when the other woman didn't answer her cell, she left the bouquet in the reception area at the shelter. Using her own key, she unlocked the kennels to walk the dogs. A couple of hours later, she'd taken all twenty-odd of them for a walk around the block. Afterwards, she visited the foster kittens. Hayley re-homed them as quickly as possible but sometimes had to ask friends to help out. So, every now and then, Aria housed foster kittens until a permanent home was found for them. Hugging a fluffy ginger kitten, she thought how special it was to have a pet. They were such characters and a never-ending source of cheer. That girl Teri could use a bit of cheer in her life. So could her handsome brother.

What a stroke of genius! How better to teach someone responsibility than by asking them to care for a helpless animal? She peered at the ginger kitten. It was adorable. Teri seemed like a lonely girl. Being forced to stay in a small town with her brother probably wasn't her idea of an ideal vacation.

Aria looked into his cute kitten eyes and smiled. "I bet you would make her summer so much better."

He mewed in response, and the impulse to take him with her grew. Teri Lockwood needed someone to love, and her brother sure as hell needed his world shaken up. Aria knew how to do both. After jotting a note for Hayley, she gathered a few things and stored them in a box along with the kitten.

"There now, baby," she assured him. "You're going to make some new friends."

It was a decent walk to the Lockwoods' house, and the kitten fussed the whole time. As she strode down the drive to the shabby porch, everything was dark except for the light filtering out from the building, which cast an eerie silvery sheen over her surroundings. She knocked promptly on the door, keen to get out of the dark as soon as possible. She plastered a grin on her face, worrying again about how she'd be received. Was she being too intrusive? Her friends would say yes. They'd tell her to mind her own business. Perhaps. Or... Maybe they'd encourage her to rock on up to his door and add some chaos to his orderly life.

Teri opened the door. Her eyes were blotchy—she'd been crying, and her mascara was smeared. When she saw Aria, she sniffed and lifted her chin. "What do you want?"

"I'm here to see Eli," Aria replied.

The box meowed. Teri stared at it, uncomprehending. Then, slowly, a smile appeared on her face, morphing her features from sullen to eager.

"Is that what I think it is?"

"Yep." Aria grinned. Whether or not Eli agreed to her crazy scheme, there was no harm in letting Teri hug the kitten. She opened the box. "Go on, give him a cuddle."

Teri lifted out the mewling ball of fur. She kissed his little nose, then cradled him to her chest and stroked his head lightly, as if she was afraid she might break him. "He's gorgeous."

But Aria wasn't looking at the kitten. A movement down the hall had drawn her attention to Eli, and her heart thudded painfully at the sight of his tall form. Teri fled into another room, taking the kitten with her.

"Hi," Eli said, leaning against the doorway and taking up entirely too much of the porch. In jeans and a tight-fitting T-shirt, he looked so casually sexy, he stole her breath. His gaze swept over her from head to toe, and then, as if he liked what he saw, the corners of his mouth crept upwards.

"Hey," Aria replied. "I know how you can teach Teri about responsibility."

"Oh?" His expression became bemused. Wary. "And how's that?"

"Hear me out," she said, rubbing her upper arms and peeking past him, wondering how she could finagle her way into the house. Even though his steady presence made the dark porch seem less ominous, she'd rather be inside. "Can I come in?"

His lips quirked. "You're asking for an invitation this time?"

"Yes." She sighed. "Are you going to hold that against me?"

He shrugged, stepping aside. "I haven't made up my mind. Come in."

She shuffled through the doorway into the hall with the faded floral wallpaper and closed the door behind her with a click.

His eyebrows squeezed together. "Now, tell me what you're on about."

Clearly, he wasn't going to offer her a cup of tea. This was as far as she'd get. His firm stance, legs spread slightly to block her from advancing, arms folded across his chest, told her that much. She eyed his thighs, appreciating the way the jeans were pulled tight across them. She swallowed and shifted her gaze to a dirty spot on the wall to the side of his shoulder.

"I volunteer at the animal shelter. Sometimes kittens are sent to foster homes until they can be permanently re-homed. Looking after one could teach Teri about being responsible."

"A kitten?" he asked incredulously. "Are you serious?"

"It would only be for a short time," she explained, her

words tripping into each other in her rush to get them out. "I know it's presumptuous, but it would be good for her."

His inhaled sharply. "What makes you think you know what's good for Therese?"

"Eli, please," Teri interrupted, emerging from a side room with the kitten in her arms. She was beaming from ear to ear. "Look at him. Isn't he so cute? Please... Can we keep him? Just for a while."

Aria sensed Eli softening. The tension in his shoulders eased, and she could tell that he was doing his best to get control of his temper. Conflicting emotions twisted his gorgeous face, and her arms ached as she suppressed the urge to wrap them around him. Her affection wouldn't be welcomed.

"Cats are hard work," he said slowly, at least considering the idea. "They need to be fed and trained to use a litter box."

"I can do that," Teri replied instantly. "It's not like I have anything else to do. Please, Eli." The expression on her face was hopeful, and he capitulated.

"It won't be forever," he warned. "Don't get too attached."

"Thank you. I won't let you down." Teri stretched onto her toes, pressed a kiss to his cheek, and vanished again.

Aria grinned, elated that he was going along with her crazy plan. "I brought over a litter box, food, worm and flea treatments," she said before he could change his mind. "The instructions are in the box."

"How did you know?" he asked. It was the last thing she'd expected him to say.

"Know what?" What direction had his mind taken?

"Therese hasn't smiled since she arrived, and she's barely spoken. You met her for ten minutes and figured out how to make her happy." His mouth turned down at the edges.

Aria fought the urge to run her finger along his lips and tug them back up again. He looked so vulnerable and uncertain, it shocked her.

"You're not mad?"

Running a hand through his hair, he sighed, and the sound was so weary, she itched to use her magic hands to work the kinks out of his back until he relaxed. The man was one big knot of stress. "No. I should be. But you made her smile. I can't take that away from her. And anyway, you're right. It will be a good lesson in responsibility."

It was perhaps the sweetest thing she'd ever heard, made all the sweeter because she sensed he didn't let his softer side show very often. He was more complicated than she'd assumed.

"She's lonely," Aria said. "I could tell."

"And you wanted to help?"

Aria drew back, studying his face, the planes and shadows of it. How was it that normal human kindness seemed strange to him? "Of course I wanted to help. I'm a nice person, Eli. This is a small town, and we do what we can to help each other out."

He stepped toward her. Taken by surprise, she moved back, and he circled around until she felt the wall hit her back and realized she was trapped between it and him.

"You're not what I expected."

His voice was low and rough. She should run away, but how could she, when staying seemed like an exciting prospect? Besides, his proximity had turned her legs to jelly, and if she tried to run, they might collapse beneath her. He leaned closer, and she caught a whiff of some expensive cologne. His nostrils flared, and she wished she'd worn perfume. It didn't seem to matter to him; his pupils dilated, and the deep blue irises ringed them, mesmerizing her.

"I live to surprise people." The breathy quality of her voice embarrassed her.

He shifted even closer, resting his arms on the wall, caging her. The position shielded his face from the light, emphasizing the hollows under his eyes and the shadow beneath his bottom lip. Her heart stuttered, and warmth flooded her.

"You should back off," Aria said more weakly than she would have liked. "I can't think straight when you're so close."

"Don't think," he replied, smoothing his palm down the side of her face, his eyes never leaving hers. His intensity unnerved her, but in a good way. She'd never met a man like him. "For a moment, just don't think."

"I can't stop." Even now, her brain was firing a million miles a minute, wondering how she'd gotten herself into this situation, what he'd do next, what she *wanted* him to do next. She couldn't forget he was a complicated, powerful man capable of destroying her, but she could pretend it didn't matter. She whispered, "Are you going to kiss me, or what?"

"Aria." Amusement tinged his voice. "You must be the least patient person I know."

She winced. "I know. It's a character flaw."

"Yes," he breathed. "I'm going to kiss you."

Then his hands fisted in her shirt, and he dragged her toward him. Her body met his and pressed flush against him, tingling in every place they touched. He was hard and strong, his chest rigid as his arms locked around her. His mouth devoured hers. This wasn't a gentle kiss, a thank-you kiss or an explorative kiss. This kiss was driven by need, and it stirred an equal response in Aria. Mouths pressed together, their tongues intertwined, dancing around each other. He took, and she gave, then turned the tide and took everything he could offer. She met him head-on. Who knew such fire hid behind his cool exterior? She moaned against his mouth.

Then he pulled away from her, and though she desperately wanted him to return, the distance between them grew. She remembered who she was. Why she couldn't do this, no matter how tempting he was, or how great at kissing. Aria stumbled out of his arms and flew out the door. Glancing over her shoulder, she saw his hands clench into fists.

"I'm sorry," he began, but she interrupted before he could continue.

"Don't worry," she said. "These things happen. It's human nature. If you'll excuse me, I've got to go. I have somewhere to be. I, uh… Good luck with the cat."

She bolted down the driveway, making an undignified exit. *Coward,* her heart screamed. *Fool,* her brain condemned.

Great. Now she was going crazy.

CHAPTER 9

A lemon cake later, Aria felt a bit better. As soon as she'd arrived home, she'd pulled out the flour, sugar and flavorings and got to work. Baking helped calm her mind, and now that she could think more clearly, she wanted to know, what had she been thinking?

She hadn't been thinking; that much was indisputable. She'd turned into mush in his arms like a big blobby marshmallow. But, god, the man could kiss. As Sophie had pointed out, it had been a long time since she'd been with a man, but she knew abstinence hadn't warped her senses that much. He was lick-your-lips, sex-on-a-stick hot, and she'd fallen under his spell. But it was over now, and even though she hadn't had the strength to resist him the first time, it couldn't happen again. She was a grown woman, capable of exercising self-control.

What was she was going to do?

She supposed she could continue exactly as she had been, print another article or two and move on. Forget about the kiss. Put her attraction to the side. It was important not to act on it, especially after seeing his other side—the side that cared about making his sister happy and was insecure about his ability to do so, the side of him that was more appealing.

After finishing a fondant daisy and placing it atop the yellow buttercream frosting, Aria stepped back to admire her work. It was midnight, and colorful creations cluttered the bench. Whenever she decorated a cake, she made a few extra sugar-paste decorations for next time. This lemon cake was destined for Saturday night dinner. Every weekend, her parents, brothers, and friends came over for a home-cooked meal. She'd begun the tradition after she moved back to Itirangi, and it had been going strong ever since. She loved being surrounded by the people she cared about and having the opportunity to catch up on gossip and interrogate any new boyfriends or girlfriends.

Flopping into a chair, she remembered what Teri had said earlier about Eli and how he'd hated the media since some fiasco with his ex. Flipping her laptop open, she clicked into Google and typed 'Elijah Lockwood', 'girlfriend', and 'scandal'. Immediately, a link to a tabloid magazine, *The Star*, appeared, with a heading which read *Socialite cheats on millionaire boyfriend with biker.*

Suddenly, the sweet scent of frosting clogging the air turned Aria's stomach. Her hand flew to her mouth. She continued reading, her horror growing as the article outlined how Eli's long-term girlfriend Victoria Burns had been sneaking around behind his back with the leader of one of Auckland's most notorious biker gangs.

No stranger to the sensationalizing of stories, Aria could have dismissed the article as unfounded, except that it contained half-a-dozen high-resolution images of a gorgeous blonde woman wrapped around a muscle-bound brute. The woman was easily recognizable, and a quick Google search for Victoria Burns confirmed her identity. Of course, the images could have been Photoshopped, but Aria doubted it. Even if someone had had the skills to create these images, Teri's earlier remark gave the article credence.

No wonder he'd disliked her from the start. If Aria's personal life had blown up as publicly as his, she'd loathe the person responsible and share his mistrust for the profession. She exited out of the article, unable to bear looking at the sordid photographs for another second. Had Eli spent hours studying them, wondering where he'd gone wrong? Had he retreated into himself when the article was released, or squared his shoulders and soldiered on? Knowing what she did of him, she suspected the latter. Her heart bled for him. But another part of her felt determined to prove to him that not all journalists were the same. Her spine straightened in steely resolution, her mind made up. She could never expose him to public ridicule or hatred in her newspaper. She'd find another way to earn her promotion. As she recalled the kiss, her hand tremored. Perhaps they could come up with something together.

Aria shut her laptop and shifted the cake she'd finished into a box, labeled the lid and slid the box onto a shelf in the pantry. Then she looked back at the bench. Flour dusted nearly every surface, and cups and spoons were strewn about as if a miniature tornado had whizzed through the kitchen. Sighing, she wiped her hands on her apron and started to clean up.

EVERY TIME ELI BLINKED, he remembered the feel of Aria's lips against his, the way her soft body had pressed into him, and the small sounds of enjoyment she'd made against his mouth. All in all, he was feeling both guilty and incredibly frustrated. Although he eased his frustration by going for a run and taking a cold shower, his guilty conscience remained.

He hadn't been gentle. What had come over him? He'd been grateful to her, yes, and she'd provoked him, but it wasn't only that. Those green flecks in her eyes had glittered. He hadn't been able to look away from her lips. And before he could think about the pros and cons, he'd kissed her. She'd tasted so good, like sweet strawberries, and he couldn't get enough.

He would have to apologize; that much was certain. Whether or not she'd asked for it, she'd looked shocked as she fled from him—for the second time, no less. Eli groaned. This apology would need more than words. Women liked flowers, didn't they? Or did they prefer chocolates? Was this something he ought to know? He didn't make a habit of being in a position where he had to apologize.

Chocolates, he decided, to satiate that sweet tooth of hers. Great, he'd come up with a plan of action. He put it to the back of his mind as he sipped his coffee and opened the paper. It was Wednesday, which meant the weekly Itirangi newsletter had arrived in the mailbox along with the *South Canterbury Chronicle*. The newsletter consisted almost entirely of notices for community meetings, book clubs and social nights, with one or two stories about local businesses thrown in. Eli read these with interest. This issue featured an article about the redheaded florist, Emily Parker, and how she'd renovated an old hotel in the town center, then rented out parts of it to other businesses. A photo dominated the front page. Eli studied it. She was pretty, something he'd noticed when they met, but she didn't stir his interest. No, his interest was reserved for a flighty brunette.

It was dangerous, his fascination with her. He hadn't taken a lover for a while, but getting involved with a local seemed like a bad idea. While it might endear him to the other locals in the short term, the opposition to his development would grow if the relationship ended badly. And any relationship between them *would* end. Eli didn't do permanent. He didn't want children, and, eventually, every woman he dated started dreaming of babies and family picnics. Either that, or they publicly humiliated him.

He grimaced. Aria wouldn't do that, but she wasn't equipped to deal with his world, and she was definitely the type to want more than a physical relationship.

The phone rang, interrupting his musings. "Lockwood."

"Elijah," his mother greeted him.

"How are you, Mother?"

"Business is going well." Frances never could tell the difference between a personal question and a business one. "How is Therese?"

"She's settling in. She doesn't want to be here, but then, you know that." After an awkward silence, the devil made him add, "She has a kitten."

"A *kitten?*" Frances spat, like it was a dirty word. "Why ever would you allow that?"

"Because she needs something to occupy her time." He winced at his defensive tone. "And it's only temporary."

She clucked her tongue. "She should invest her time more wisely. Learn a language, perhaps."

"Mother, she's a teenage girl," he exclaimed, exasperated. "Do you really expect that to happen?"

"I expect her to fulfill her obligations."

Taking a deep breath, he counted to ten in his head. Frances riled him, and he had to be careful not to get too worked up. "Why did you call?"

A beat of silence. Then: "Can't a mother call her own children?"

"Not you," he replied. "Not without a good reason."

Her impatience was perceptible through the phone line. "Your father and I are in Christchurch for business," she said. "We're coming over for dinner tonight."

A visit was unexpected. Especially so soon after he'd last seen her. "Will you stay?" he asked.

69

"No. We'll only be there for a couple of hours."

"When should I expect you?" He needed to prepare.

He could almost hear her check her watch. "We're about to leave."

It was three o'clock. After a quick goodbye, he hung up and glanced around. The dining room was a shambles, and his parents would expect it to be tidy and clean. They'd also expect a decent meal, which wasn't likely to happen. He needed to buy takeaways or hire a chef. Of the two, takeaways would be by far the cheaper and easier option, but his parents would no doubt turn their noses up at it. He'd have to find a caterer. This visit of theirs was going to be far more hassle than it was worth.

CHAPTER 10

*T*here were no catering companies in the phone book. None. Eli rang two local cafés and the famous bakehouse, which he had yet to visit, but none of them did private catering. In addition to that, neither of the cafés could spare any staff, and the baker refused to help, cursing Eli in a thick German accent for daring to introduce mass-market baked goods to the township. Not that he had done so yet, but when asked, he couldn't deny that a couple of well-known chain bakeries were interested in renting shop space from him. Eli was, apparently, notorious among a certain set of locals.

He searched the Internet for caterers, but nothing in this backwards little town was on the web. Finally, he called the pub.

The Irish bartender answered. "Davy of Davy's speaking. What can I do you for?"

"I need a caterer," Eli replied, thinking he might have more luck if he didn't mention his name. "Tonight. I know it's short notice, but I was wondering if you know of anybody."

"Who's asking?"

"Eli," he replied.

"Eli who?"

"Lockwood," he said impatiently. There went that plan.

"Ri-i-ight. I remember you." Davy's voice had taken on a sly tone that Eli didn't much like. "You've got a thing for our Aria." Eli didn't have time to correct him before he barreled on. "Well, tonight's your lucky night, my friend."

Eli's heart sank. "Why?"

"We don't have any professional caterers in town, but we do have a couple of bloody good home-cooks who cook for fundraisers from time to time. Your lady friend is one of them."

Eli sighed. So much for hiring a caterer to make his life easier. Involving Aria would never simplify things, and after she had run from him twice, it seemed unlikely she'd be willing to help.

"Anyone else?" He crossed his fingers.

Davy seemed puzzled but answered anyway. "Nancy Harding, but she's visiting her niece in Wanaka at the moment, and Eliza Brown."

"Do you have Mrs. Brown's number?"

Davy gave him the number but made sure to tell him Aria's as well. Eli called the first number.

"Eliza speaking."

"Mrs. Brown," he began. "This is Elijah Lockwood." No point in trying to hide his identity again. "I hear you're a good cook."

"Yes." The old woman sounded wary.

"Would you consider catering for a dinner tonight? I know it's short notice, but I'm desperate. You can name your price." Hopefully, adding a financial incentive would aid his cause.

She took her time answering. "I'm afraid I'm otherwise engaged tonight, Mr. Lockwood. Your best bet is to call Miss Aria Simons. I'm sure you know her."

Was he paranoid, or were the locals pushing him toward the feisty journalist?

"I do," he replied. "Are you sure I can't persuade you?"

"No, Mr. Lockwood. Not tonight."

He sighed. "Then I'll give her a call. Thank you for your time."

∼

Aria was dozing off in the back corner of a workshop about public transportation when her phone rang, jolting her back to consciousness. Leaping at the chance to escape the workshop, which was going nowhere fast, she excused herself and accepted the call.

"Hey, there," she greeted cheerfully.

"Aria, this is Eli."

His smooth voice sent a ripple of desire down her spine, and she flashed back to their kiss last night. Her body temperature ratcheted up a couple of degrees.

"Hi, Eli," she greeted him, doing her best to sound nonchalant despite her racing heart. Was he calling about last night? Did he want to talk about it? Apologize? Ask for more? She wasn't sure which option she'd prefer. "Can I help you?"

"Davy the bartender tells me you're a 'bloody good cook'. His words, not mine."

She laughed. Typical of Davy to talk her up to an unattached man. "Is that a question or a statement?"

"Are you?"

"Yes," she replied, tucking a curl behind her ear as she pressed the phone closer to prevent anyone around her overhearing. "I'm a passable cook."

"Are you free tonight?"

"Are you asking me on a date?" she teased. Sensing his awkwardness, she said, "I'm sorry. I was joking."

"I need a caterer."

Oh. Not quite a date, then. Couldn't blame a girl for dreaming. "What for?"

He paused. Sighed. What was bugging him? "My parents are coming to dinner."

Aria laughed out loud. "And you need a caterer for that? Seriously, roast some potatoes and a chicken, and they'll be happy."

"I wish it were that simple."

Aria shook her head. He made it sound like he belonged to the Addams Family. Even if they weren't like her family, they couldn't be that bad. Was this a ruse to see her again? She hoped so; otherwise, he seriously needed to relax.

"It's always that simple with family," she advised. "Make a little effort, and they'll appreciate it."

"Not my parents," he said shortly. "I didn't call to get your opinion. I need a caterer. Will you do it?"

His tone was snappy, and she couldn't help feeling hurt. "Well, I could have been, but now I'm not so sure."

"I'll pay you."

She groaned and raked a hand down her face. "Not every-thing is about money, Eli."

"Then name your price."

She hesitated, seeing the opportunity that had dropped into her lap. "Information," she replied, in control once more. "I need a killer article. Something big. Exclusive, but not scandalous. Can you help me with that?"

For twenty seconds, she thought he'd tell her to go to hell. Wouldn't blame him if he did.

"What kind of story?"

He was listening to her, at least. "Anything that will sell papers."

"You don't care about the content?"

She shook her head. "Not as long as it's worth my time."

She heard his breathing down the phone. Then he said,

"Okay, deal. But if you write anything I don't agree to, I'll make you pay for it."

The threat should have bothered her, but it didn't. Perhaps because she'd seen him kowtow to his little sister only the night before, or because she knew the reason for his reluctance. "Agreed. I'll help with your meal. I can be there at five and have dinner done by six-thirty. Does that suit?"

"Yes." He exhaled softly. "Thank you. Is there anything I need to buy?"

"Two dozen potatoes and a block of cheese." Deathly silence. Winding him up was such fun, but he clearly wasn't in the mood for jokes. "How do you like Italian? I can cook pumpkin ravioli, risotto, and lemon cake for dessert. No need to buy anything. I have everything I need at home." She'd have to sacrifice the family cake, but she'd happily give up ten such cakes to get the story she needed.

"That sounds fantastic." His voice had warmed considerably, and she found she liked it.

Aria grinned. "You'll make it worthwhile, I'm sure. Now, I'd better get back to work. See you later."

At five o'clock, Aria turned up on Eli's doorstep with several bags of food and a big smile. Eli wondered if she ever stopped smiling.

"One caterer, as promised," she announced, pushing past him to unload the bags in the kitchen, her calves sleek as she bounced along the hall in chunky high heels.

"I'm so glad you could help," he said, regardless of the price he'd pay for her assistance. He needed her on-side tonight. Family dinners were, frankly, unpleasant. Hopefully, she would cook a great meal and stay away from his parents. The last thing he needed was for her to bring up their kiss in front of them. On that note...

"I bought you some chocolates," he told her, grabbing the box from the bench and handing it over.

"Do you think you can buy my goodwill with chocolates?" she asked, laughing.

"Of course not. I need to apologize for last night. I got carried away, and I'm sorry."

"Wow." Her eyebrows shot up as she scanned the box. "Good choice. Creamy and chocolatey. Perfect. How did you know?"

Eli smiled as her approval sent a tingle of pleasure through him. Most women of his acquaintance weren't easily pleased. Many things about Aria were refreshing. She was colorful and cheerful and passionate. Nice to look at, too. The women he usually met tended to be elegant and sophisticated—tall and lean, whereas Aria was average height and delightfully proportioned. Today, a V-necked summer dress displayed her ample curves to perfection.

"They're my favorite," he confessed.

She opened the box and offered him one, then popped another into her own mouth and closed her eyes dreamily. "So good."

Eli gritted his teeth as the gooey inside of the chocolate melted in his mouth. How did she make the simple act of eating so sensual? He swallowed. "We'll be eating in the dining room. Do you need anything before you get started?"

"No, I've got everything sorted. Don't worry," she added, seeing the apprehension on his face. "It'll be fine. Go and be with your parents."

He headed back to the dining room, which he'd cleaned and filled with a large oak table, which stretched nearly the entire length of the room. His parents and Therese had congregated at the end nearest to the fireplace—not that it was burning, with the warm summer air.

"Dinner will be ready in an hour or so," he informed them.

"I assume you've hired a cook?" Frances asked, as if the idea of cooking for themselves was inconceivable.

"Yes, Mother. She came highly recommended." So highly recommended, it made him suspicious.

"Nothing but the best for my children," Phillip commented.

An hour passed in stilted conversation until Aria emerged with the ravioli. A patterned apron covered her summer dress, and she had a spot of flour on her cheek. Eli wanted to lick it off. Then his mouth watered for a different reason. Damn, the ravioli smelled good.

"Aria," Therese exclaimed. "What are you doing here?"

"Cooking your dinner." Her eyes slid nervously toward Eli's parents, then back to Therese. "How's the kitten?"

"He's fab. I've named him Aroha," Therese replied. "Because I love him. He's soooo cute. He slept on my bed last night."

Frances and Phillip both frowned, and Eli gestured for Therese to stop talking. Their parents weren't partial to pets and were no doubt looking for somebody to blame for the kitten.

"I'm glad it worked out." Aria wound around the table, placing a bowl of ravioli before each of them. Everyone waited while Phillip tasted the first bite.

"Delicious," he said after a painful five seconds.

Aria beamed and scurried from the room. Eli felt oddly proud of her, a strange warmth in the vicinity of his chest. He shouldn't be surprised that the woman could cook. She also saved kittens and stopped stupid girls from getting a criminal record. What didn't she do?

The best surprise was dessert, a beautifully decorated yellow cake. Three tiers high, spotted with edible daisies and butterflies, it was a work of art.

"Did you do this yourself?" Eli asked, unable to mask his approval.

A smile elevated her face from simply pretty to beautiful. "Yes, I did," she replied. "I'm a bit of an amateur cake decorator."

"It looks divine," Frances said. "Lacking the flair of a true professional, but no one would expect you to reach their standard, dear."

Eli rolled his eyes. So like his mother to deliver a backhanded compliment.

"Thank you," Aria said simply, and he admired her graceful acceptance of the comment. She handled herself well, better than he would have thought. "Do you need anything else from me?"

"No," he said. "I'll see you out."

"I'm sure she can see herself out," Frances interjected.

"I can," Aria confirmed, looking as if she'd like nothing better.

"Nevertheless," Eli continued. "I will see you out." He stood and, taking her elbow, escorted her to the front door. When they reached the porch, his grip tightened. "Thank you for saving me tonight," he murmured, gazing down into her bottomless brown eyes, aware of her bare skin against his fingers as he rubbed a thumb over her elbow, so smooth and so soft. "I know you'll probably milk me for all I'm worth, but I want you to know that I really appreciate your help anyway. I would have been stuck without you."

Aria smiled, her eyes twinkling. "You're very welcome, Eli Lockwood. I'll come by to talk to you tomorrow, if that suits."

"I'm looking forward to it." And, oddly, he was.

Before he could second-guess himself, Eli leaned over and kissed her cheek. She blushed deep red and hurried away, waving to him before she hopped into her car, a ridiculous little thing with a flower painted on the side. Taking a deep breath to fortify himself, he went back into the lion's den.

CHAPTER 11

*W*hen Aria called Eli the next day, she got the answer phone and left a brief message. Later that afternoon, she was sitting at her desk banging out an article about a member of the Bridge Club who'd won a tournament up north when a disturbance at the other end of the office caught her attention. While newspaper offices were indisputably chaotic at the best of times, she was familiar with the particular brand of chaos belonging to the *South Canterbury Chronicle,* so when it became hushed, she immediately noticed. Curiosity got the better of her, and she craned her neck to see what was going on.

Eli was standing just inside the door, dressed for work in a suit that fitted perfectly, with a blue silk tie knotted around his neck. He was cradling a bouquet of pink roses and a bouquet of red roses in the crook of his arm. Every female in the room had stopped to stare at him. One or two swooned. When he caught sight of Aria, a grin spread across his face. She swallowed, mouth dry. He started toward her with purpose.

"Hi, Eli," she called as he drew closer.

"Hi, yourself." He settled on the seat she kept for guests and handed her the bouquets.

Her eyebrows shot up. "What are these for?"

"To say thank you."

"They're lovely, but you didn't need to. We have a deal, remember?"

He shoved his hand into his pocket. "I wanted to. Deal or not."

"Seriously. No one has given me flowers since the high school dance." Which was sad, now that she came to think of it.

She leaned over to read the card. *Thank you for improving an awful night.* How sweet. Roses would have been romantic, coming from someone else. From Eli Lockwood, they unsettled her. She didn't understand him and didn't know what he wanted. He kissed like she was his last salvation, then pushed her away. He was powerful in business, but vulnerable when it came to family. The man was a puzzle, and she wasn't sure whether she wanted to figure him out.

"If I didn't know better, I'd think you liked me."

"Maybe I do. Is that such a bad thing?" He held up a hand. "Wait—don't answer that. I don't think my ego can handle it."

She chuckled. "I think your ego could withstand a nuclear blast."

He tilted his head, neither agreeing nor disagreeing, then rolled his shoulders inside the immaculate charcoal suit. "Okay, you have me at your mercy. Hit me with the questions."

She steepled her fingers. "You're meant to be giving *me* a story, remember?"

He watched her, almost preternaturally still except for his lips, which were twitching. She thought about kissing him. Reminded herself that men like him were bad for women like her.

"I thought you'd at least have some idea where to start."

She wished she did. She needed this promotion. But short of reaffirming for him that journalists had no morals, she wasn't sure exactly how he could give her a story. Closing her eyes, she felt the usual rush of shame that came whenever she remembered *The Press* and Wilson Jones. Anger chased the shame away. She shouldn't have to feel ashamed when she had done nothing wrong. But this promotion would certainly help to prove that fact to others.

"Let's say I've got nothing. What have you done recently which might be newsworthy? Is there anything I've missed in my other articles? Big-name brands interested in buying into your development?" She'd slipped into interview mode. The questions spilled forth. "Any changes you plan to make, based on opposition from some locals? Any possibility you've fallen in love with the town and plan to move here permanently?"

The last question was a joke. Almost.

"Erm." He mulled it over for a moment. "A few chain stores have expressed interest, but none are confirmed. I haven't decided what kind of tenants I'd like yet. Every development is different, and you only get one chance to do it right."

"Sounds like doing it right matters a lot to you." She was fishing, trying to figure out what made him tick.

"It does. Every place needs something a little different from the others. I still haven't got to the heart of what Itirangi needs yet."

She played devil's advocate. "I wouldn't have thought what Itirangi needs would factor into your decision-making."

He huffed and looked at her as though she should know better. She couldn't help noticing he was more talkative than when she'd previously interviewed him. Perhaps he trusted her more. *Or perhaps*, she thought wryly, *it's simply a matter of being on the front foot this time*.

"Could you let me in on who you're considering?" she asked.

"Dunkin' Donuts and Starbucks have both approached me," he said slowly, as if he was uncertain how much to reveal. "As have Hannah's Shoes, Witchery, and Forever New. I've also had inquiries from a couple of designer brands—Gucci and Louis Vuitton—but they're still on the fence. You may be surprised to learn this, but a number of local businesses have also asked me about having a storefront."

"*Really?*" Aria leaned forward, ignoring the aroma of the roses, which was tickling her nostrils. "That *is* news. Do you mind if I publish any of this?"

He shook his head. "Thank you for asking."

"Of course." She asked a number of follow-up questions, scrawling shorthand notes on a brightly colored piece of memo paper. Finally, she thought she had enough for another article. Maybe not the Big Story she'd hoped for, but better than what she'd had before his visit. "Thanks for holding up your end of the deal."

"Anytime."

Warmth flooded his voice, and she glanced up to find him watching her with the oddest expression. On anyone else, she'd call it indulgent. Affectionate. On him, she was at a loss.

"You did me a huge favor yesterday," he said. "I'm glad to be able to pay it back. And now that we're even, I'm hoping you'll agree to another one."

Butterflies invaded her stomach. What more could he want from her? Her mind fired off with dirty ideas. She tried to shake them loose. "Eli—"

"Just hear me out," he interrupted, as if he hadn't heard her.

Okay. She could do that.

"I'd like you to help Therese."

"Excuse me?" Of all the favors she might have expected, this hadn't even made the list.

He winced and ran a hand through his hair distractedly, then stood, paced away from her desk and back again. "I don't know what to do. I'm at a loss. She responded well to you, and she needs a good female role model."

"Me? A role model?" Every time he opened his mouth, he said something that shocked her. The idea of being a role model was totally inconceivable when one knew her past. Or at least, what others perceived to be her past.

"Don't make me say what you already know," he grumbled, incorrectly assuming she was seeking compliments. "You're well-educated, with a career and a social life. You embrace your femininity rather than rejecting it like my mother does. She makes Therese think it's not okay to act like a girl."

Well. Who would have guessed he thought so highly of her? How flattering. Something in her tummy buzzed happily. She found herself asking, "What can I do?"

He resumed his pacing. "You'll help her?"

Aria kicked herself internally even as she said, "Yes. I like Teri. I don't want to get your hopes up, though. I'm not a miracle worker."

"I don't need you to work miracles," he said. "Just be yourself. Do girl stuff with her."

She rolled her eyes and tucked an errant strand of hair behind her ear. "That's so vague."

He frowned in consternation. "Take her shopping. Get your nails done. Whatever it is that girls do to bond."

"I can see you're an expert on female bonding." She laughed at his befuddled expression. "Leave it up to me. But my first piece of advice is that you need to call her Teri."

He frowned again, eyebrows knitted tightly above bewildered blue eyes. "Her name is Therese."

Did he really know so little about women? "She introduced herself to me as Teri, which means it's the name she prefers. Calling her Therese won't win you any points."

"Okay," he said slowly, nodding. "I'll do my best. Thank you. I would never have known that."

"It's my job to read people," she said. "Don't feel too badly about it."

"There's no need for you to be concerned about my feelings," he said wryly. "I'm a terrible brother. I know that. One other thing: I'd appreciate it if you didn't let her know I asked you to help. I don't want her to feel like a charity case."

"Duly noted."

He moved closer, and she slouched back, keeping her breathing even, unwilling to let him know how he affected her. Then, when his deep blue eyes bored into hers, she couldn't look away. Fortunately, he didn't seem to have the same problem as he broke eye contact and shucked his jacket, the epitome of casual elegance.

"I'd like to repay you for helping," he said. "Can I take you to dinner tonight?"

Definitely a bad idea. It would make people see fire where there was only smoke. "Sorry, I'm busy tonight."

"Tomorrow?" he asked.

"I've got a family dinner."

"Are you always busy?"

She smiled. "More or less."

"Name a time and place. I'm free most evenings for as long as I'm here."

Aria couldn't understand his persistence. "I'll keep that in mind." She tilted her head toward the exit. "I'd better get to work. I have a living to earn." She turned her computer on, ignoring the painful thumping in her chest, which told her he hadn't moved.

"You won't forget about Therese?"

"Teri," she reminded him. "I'll call her later. Have a good day, Eli."

He handed her a card with a number on it and made for the exit. She breathed a sigh of relief before picking up the phone.

"Hi, Teri," she said when the teenager answered the phone. "It's Aria here."

"Hey." Teri sounded pleased to hear from her, but also wary, like her brother.

"Would you like to get out of the house on Saturday?" Aria asked. "It's meant to be nice weather, and there's a beach at Timaru, about forty minutes from here. What do you say?"

There was a pause. "It beats watching TV."

"Great. I'll pick you up at eleven. See you then."

And now, finally, she could get to work.

ARIA AND SOPHIE met for lunch at the bakehouse, where they ran through the events of the morning and the previous night.

"He's interested in you," Sophie said bluntly.

"He is *not*," Aria protested. She was sure of it. Perhaps he was physically attracted to her—she'd allow that—but a guy like him couldn't really see anything in a girl like her. She was provincial. He was wealthy, handsome and powerful. Still, she couldn't help wondering: What would it be like if he *was* into her? The man was a magician with his lips—two days later, their kiss was still fresh in her mind. She'd bet his hands had the same level of expertise.

Sophie was devouring a chocolate croissant. "Let's look at the facts," she said between bites. "The man bought you a drink, groped you in public, kissed you, and then invited you to cook for his parents. Yeah, you're right. It doesn't seem like he's interested."

Aria shook her head slightly, amused by her friend's liberal use of sarcasm. "You're making it sound different than it is."

"You have to admit, he is a sexy beast."

Amen to that. Whatever his faults, Eli was an extremely

handsome man. Even though it annoyed her that Sophie thought so too.

They parted ways, Aria's thoughts occupied by images of Eli's handsome face leaning closer to her, his lips alighting on her cheek in the lightest of kisses. Drat Sophie and her talk of sexy beasts. She headed back to her office only to be accosted by Eliza Brown at the door.

"I hear you're involved with the developer," Eliza croaked.

"I'm not," Aria said firmly, hoping she wasn't blushing from the fantasies which had whirled through her mind moments earlier. "We've worked together a couple of times. That's all."

Eliza's wizened face crinkled around the eyes. "That's not ideal. The articles you published haven't stopped the development from progressing. I was of the belief, Miss Simons, that you have a history of using unconventional methods to succeed."

If she'd wanted to press the right buttons, she'd succeeded. Aria hated nothing more than remembering what so many people still thought of her. Shame clawed at her gut again, and she rubbed her temples. Could she never escape the gossip?

"Don't believe everything you hear, Eliza. I never promised to stop this development, and I haven't done the things people say I have. I'm not that girl."

I never was.

ELI CALLED Mark while he was driving back to the villa he shared with Teri. He was about to do something he wasn't quite comfortable with, but it needed to be done, and he'd never before hesitated to do what was necessary.

"Hi, Eli," Mark greeted him. "How are you?"

"Fine," he answered shortly. "I need you to investigate someone for me."

"No pleasantries?" Mark asked. "You used to call me because you liked talking to me. What happened to those days?"

"You got old and boring," Eli replied, knowing that if either of them had become boring, it certainly wasn't Mark, who lived a high-flying lifestyle.

"Yes, well, you could try to be social instead of only calling to order me around."

His friend was teasing, but it struck close to home. "I'll tell you what—I'll call you this weekend so we can talk about our feelings. For now, I need your professional help."

"What do you need me to do?"

"There's a reporter," Eli said. "I'm worried about her."

"Of course you are." Mark's tone became serious. "What does she want?"

"Nothing, at the moment. But it's best to be cautious."

"Always. You want me to crush her?"

"No." Eli cursed himself for being so obvious.

"Is this reporter young and pretty?" Mark asked. "Has she got you wrapped around her finger?"

"No, but we've got an understanding, and I don't see any reason to mess with her livelihood."

"So, what do you want me to do?" Mark's confusion was evident.

"Look into her background. See if there are any secrets hiding in her dirty laundry."

"I'm a lawyer, not a private investigator," Mark reminded him. "That's not my job."

"Get one of your underlings to do it, but get it done."

"Eli..." Mark began, then hesitated before continuing. "Are you sure this is work-related? If you're interested in her on a personal level, this isn't the way to go."

"It's not personal." Eli scowled at the phone. "I'm protecting my business."

"Then consider it done. Send me her details."

He did, like a total cad. He'd asked for Aria's help, and she'd kindly agreed. Investigating her in this way seemed wrong, but he quashed his reservations. It was necessary, just to make sure she was exactly how she painted herself.

"Be careful," Mark warned him. "If this girl finds out you're investigating her, anything between you will be over." Then he disconnected the call.

Eli tried to convince himself that he was doing the right thing, but digging into Aria's past while using her to help with his sister didn't seem right. On any level.

CHAPTER 12

*W*hen Teri opened the door to Aria on Saturday morning, she was decked out in a black mini-dress with boots and dark makeup.

"I've got my bikini on underneath. Is that all right?" she asked anxiously.

"That's great," Aria replied. "So do I." It was a beautiful day, with the sun beaming down and only a few fluffy clouds floating in the sky. Perfect for swimming. "Shall we get going?"

Teri hesitated, glancing back into the house. "Uh, actually, my brother is coming with us, if that's okay."

Great, more time with Mr. Hottie—the same Mr. Hottie who wanted to take her on a date. Aria began re-thinking her choice of swimsuit. Usually, she was comfortable in the purple halter-neck bikini, but it did show off a lot of skin. That wouldn't help maintain the distance needed from Eli.

"It's fine," Aria said, ignoring her misgivings. "The more the merrier."

"Glad to hear that," Eli said, appearing in the doorway.

"So, you're coming with us." She tried to look more enthusiastic than she felt.

"If I won't be intruding."

Aria gave him the once-over. Was he going for casual? His lips kept twitching, and he sounded stiffer than a board. The slacks and open-necked shirt he was sporting had probably cost more than all the shoes she owned, and she owned *a lot* of shoes.

"Of course, you're welcome to come," she said. "As long as you realize there'll be a spot of shopping before the beach." She didn't know what devil had driven her to adjust their plans, but it was probably the same one that was desperate to see how Eli would handle a situation outside of his control.

To his credit, Eli winced but didn't falter. "I could do with a new pair of shoes."

That was a massive fib if ever she'd heard one. His handmade leather shoes were in perfect condition. She'd bet that he polished them every night before bed. "Come on, then." She waved at her car.

Eli groaned. "This isn't a car, it's a golf cart."

"It's Betty," she corrected, patting the vehicle's bonnet fondly. "And she prefers not to be referred to as a golf cart. She's perfectly adequate."

"Yes, for one tiny person. Not for all three of us. We'll take my car. It's roomier."

Aria didn't move. "Get in," she said. "This is our girls' day, and we're doing it my way."

"Fine." He raised his hands in a gesture of surrender. "But I get the front seat."

Aria and Teri stared at him.

"Okay, I'll go in the back."

Teri burst out laughing.

"What?" he demanded.

"Nothing," she replied hurriedly. "Only, I've never seen you get bossed around by anyone other than Mum and Dad."

"Don't get used to it."

With a scowl of displeasure, he squeezed into the back

seat. Aria smiled, taking the driver's seat. It was going to be a long day, but at least they'd gotten off on the right foot.

∾

"Timaru is perched on the rim of an extinct volcano." Aria was playing tour guide as they drove through the outer suburbs. "Mount Horrible. Nice, huh? There are just over thirty-five thousand people here. In Itirangi, we tend to think of Timaru as a city, but it's really only a town."

The residential area they had passed through on the outskirts of Timaru was hilly, while the central business district they were now emerging into was flatter. Out of the window, Eli could see hotels and houses perched on a craggy cliff which overlooked the ocean.

"That's where the rich folks live," she explained. "Some of them, at least. Wouldn't want to be them in thirty years, when the cliff has eroded and they fall into the water."

Aria's first stop was a clothing store. The girls hurried inside. Eli followed, looking grim. It felt like four hours later when he finally escaped, having learned that an hour spent listening to women chat about which colors flattered certain complexions seemed much longer.

It was all *her* fault. That brightly colored, too-perky, infuriating woman. She'd done it on purpose, to drive him crazy. He'd seen it in her eyes.

But now it was over, thank god, and they could relax on the beach. Eli enjoyed the beach. An excellent surfer, he thrived on the thrill of flying through the waves and the calm of lying on the sand. In winter, he often needed to wear a wetsuit, but he hadn't bothered to pack one today. It was warm enough not to need one.

He probably shouldn't have come. He should have let Aria and Teri bond, but he'd read the article Aria had written about his development in the morning paper, and it had

91

stunned him. Simple and honest. What surprised him further was that she hadn't yet published anything personal about him. She was leaving him out of it. He should be pleased about that. Usually, he preferred to keep any interest focused on his company and away from himself, but for some reason, he wanted to believe Aria saw the man behind the business— that she was interested in Elijah Lockwood, person, as much as Elijah Lockwood, CEO.

The two words she had afforded him in the morning's article were 'efficient' and 'ambitious'. Both were true, but he was more than that—something he wanted to her to know. And so here he was, standing next to a ridiculously small car, waiting on two troublesome females.

Aria turned to him and smiled slyly. "We're not done yet," she said. "We've more shops to look at."

"What?"

"A few more shops," she repeated, like it was the most reasonable thing in the world.

"You've just been shopping."

"For casual clothes," Therese chimed in, looking far too pleased with herself. "Aria promised we could go shopping for dresses too. But you don't have to come. We're fine by ourselves."

Eli was baffled. Was this an invitation to come, or a warning not to? "I'll tell you what," he said, thinking quickly. "Why don't you two finish shopping, and I'll walk down to the beach. You can meet me there when you're done."

"Do you know how to get to the beach?" Aria asked.

"I'm the CEO of a successful business," he replied. "I can figure it out."

"He won't ask for directions," Teri muttered.

Aria nodded. "Men never do."

Biting back a retort, he stalked off. Aria's proclamations and proclivity for teasing made him want to growl or argue her into submission, but doing so would be counterproductive. As long as he continued to surprise her, he would have the upper hand.

Eli found the beach easily. The town center arched around it, with shops and cafés overlooking the sea. A boardwalk meandered through the low sand dunes so the infirm and elderly could stroll along the beach more easily. Native grasses grew in clumps, and a sign at the beginning of the boardwalk indicated that blue penguins nested under the path and could be seen returning to their nests from the water at dusk. The sand, which was tan rather than white, squished beneath his toes. A few toddlers were building sand castles along the shore, and groups of teenagers were basking in the sun or splashing in the shallows. Two windsurfers were gliding across the bay. Eli untied his shoes and left them on the sand as he stepped into the water. It lapped over his feet, cool but not cold, and turquoise in color rather than the blue waters of the beaches back home.

He walked along the edge of the surf to a stall renting out surfboards and requested one. The waves were calm, and gulls were crying overhead. He cruised the waves for an hour and was toweling off when he caught sight of two things: the first, Teri, in a tiny bikini, strolling past a group of ogling, catcalling teenage boys. His fists clenched, and before he knew it, he was yelling, "Jesus Christ! Get hold of yourselves!"

The second was Aria, in a similarly small bikini, showing off an expanse of smooth olive skin. She'd tied her hair in a knot and she was laughing, head thrown back. His gaze moved up long legs that he imagined wrapping around him to a slightly curved stomach with flared hips and a narrow waist and stopped at the halter top, which showed off her fantastic cleavage. He wanted to run his hands over those curves and feel their softness. He gulped, suddenly very glad he was still holding the surfboard in front of him.

What was she thinking? He'd asked her to set a good example for Therese. She needed to cover up. *He* needed to cover her up. Desperately. Looking around for something to use, Eli saw a towel on the sand and retrieved it. At her side in a few strides, he tossed it over her.

"What the hell?" she demanded, eyes flashing angrily.

Hmm. How to explain this? "You're setting a bad example," he said. "That bikini is microscopic."

"I'm setting a bad example because I'm proud of my body?"

If she had been a dog, her hackles would be raised. Perhaps a different tack was in order. "You're drawing attention to yourself."

"Have you considered that maybe I like the attention?"

Well, no. He hadn't.

"Anyway, you're drawing more attention to me by being so overdramatic."

It was true. At least a dozen people were listening to their discussion but pretending not to.

"Fine," he grumped. "Please yourself."

She dropped the towel on the sand and stomped on it. "I will." Then she slunk away, leaving him with a hard-on and a sinking feeling.

"God, Eli. You're so uncool," Therese exclaimed, her face flaming with embarrassment. The ground he'd made up with her was slipping away.

"You look really nice," he said weakly.

Therese turned up her nose and stalked toward the water, following Aria. One of the teenage boys sniggered. Eli glared at him. It didn't seem to have any effect.

"Bro, you are so dead," the kid told him.

Eli closed his eyes and groaned. "I know."

CHAPTER 13

*M*icroscopic! She scoffed. As if. Her bikini was *perfectly* appropriate. Who cared what he thought, anyway? If not for him, she and Teri could have looked good and flirted with the beach-goers. If *he* hadn't come along, they could be having a great time. What the hell had he meant by throwing a towel over her? How rude. And how awful. Tears pricked her eyes. She blinked them back. She'd worked too hard at being comfortable with herself to let one stupid man ruin it.

That he looked absolutely magnificent wasn't fair. She hadn't noticed him when they'd started making their way to the water, but when she did, *Oh boy*. Never before had a naked chest affected her so much. He must have recently exited the water, because droplets were glistening on his strong shoulders and corded biceps. Rivulets ran down his broad chest and trickled into the deep groove in the middle of his abdomen. The damp hair on his torso was springy, and she wanted to run her fingers through it.

He was physically perfect. And it irked her.

Aria had never been perfect. A chubby teenager, she'd only slimmed down once she discovered the gym at university and began giving her cakes away rather than eating them all herself. She'd never be thin, though. Her shoulders were square and her hips were wide, the skin laced with fine silver stretch marks which had persisted through every quack remedy she'd tried to fade them away. Apparently, she had a genetic predisposition for them. Just her luck. Still, they weren't visible from a distance, so she'd decided not to worry.

After seeing the physical perfection of Eli Lockwood, however, she wished, just a little bit, that her blemishes would disappear.

"Eli is so lame," Teri said, catching up to her. "He thinks it's all right for him to be shirtless but gets angry at us for wearing bikinis? What a jerk."

"Don't worry about it," Aria replied. "He's just old-fashioned."

That thought brought on a vision of Eli emerging from a lake, Mr. Darcy style. *Bad, Ri.*

Teri scowled. "I think we look hot."

"So do I." Aria wasn't about to teach a teenage girl to be insecure about her body. The world had enough self-doubting girls already. "Do you like swimming?"

Teri shrugged noncommittally. "It's okay, but I suck at it."

Interesting, then, that her brother enjoyed surfing. He couldn't have picked the hobby up from their parents.

"Would you rather swim or sunbathe?"

"I might get some sun," Teri said, studying the water as it rolled in to shore.

Aria followed her gaze wistfully, imagining the cool water splashing over her skin. It was too warm to bake on the beach. But she was here to spend time with Teri.

"I'll join you," she said.

Teri laughed. "Don't be stupid. You totally want to swim. Go for it. I don't give a shit."

"Are you sure?" Aria was already turning toward the water.

"Yeah." Teri laid a towel out on the sand and sat on it, then leaned back with her hands behind her head. As soon as she was settled, Aria made a beeline for the water and sighed happily when it flowed over her toes. She ran at the next wave and jumped into it head first, like she always did. Better to deal with the shock of being submerged in cold water all at once rather than gradually. She rose out of the water and laughed, shaking droplets from her hair, then stretched out and jumped in again, this time swimming until she reached the end of the bay.

AFTER HER SWIM, Aria lounged on a towel in the sun to dry off. Teri had wandered away with a cute boy she planned to go on a movie date with. A shadow fell over Aria, and a drop of cool water landed on her face. Shielding her eyes from the sun, she peered up and drooled over six feet of half-naked man. A shiver passed over her chest. Her mouth dried out. She *had* to stop having this reaction to him; it was ridiculous.

"Can I sit?" he asked, gesturing to the spot beside her.

"Go for it. It's a free country." Maybe she was still a little pissed off at him for his weird behavior earlier. He sank down next to her, smelling of salt and sweat. The Mr. Darcy fantasy returned. She sighed, wishing Teri were here to act as a buffer between them.

"I shouldn't have thrown the towel at you," he said abruptly.

Aria raised herself up on her elbows. "Was that an apology?"

He turned to her with a wry smile. "More like an admission. I don't apologize well."

"So, that's as close as I'm going to get?"

"Yes."

"Hmph." She nibbled on her lower lip, thinking how damned sexy he looked in board shorts. Made it easy to forget how uptight he was. Also easy to forget all the reasons she shouldn't encourage his attention. "Hmm."

"What?" he asked, mildly irritated.

"That's not good enough."

He growled. "What do you want from me?"

Aria knew *exactly* what she wanted from him. Their mind-blowing kiss was still on her mind. But she couldn't ask for that. She wasn't bold enough, or stupid enough.

"I want you to kiss me," she whispered. Apparently, her brain hadn't gotten the memo. His eyes widened and darkened, then he shut them tightly. Was it desire she'd seen burning in them? She thought so. Good; she wanted to melt his cool façade. At the same time, she knew it was a terrible idea. "And I want you to touch me." The words were coming from a seductress who had taken over her body. She couldn't believe anything else. What was it about him that made her reckless? "I want to feel your skin against mine," the seductress continued.

Eli tensed—whether to pounce or flee, she wasn't sure. Driven by a crazy impulse, she reached over and traced a finger down his taut stomach, discovering that the ridges of his muscles were hot steel covered by hotter flesh.

He gasped when she touched him. "You're driving me crazy," he said. "God, Aria."

Spurred on by his reaction, she smoothed her palm up his arm, feeling the firm bicep and strong shoulder. The feel of his hot skin inspired thoughts in Aria that she'd never expected to have. Fantasies of rubbing against his superb body in bed, luxuriating in the sensation of his heat covering her.

Aria had only slept with two people—both long-term boyfriends—and she'd been in a sexual drought for a long time. She was overdue for some nookie. Maybe it was time for her to be a little wild. Powerful men could ruin lives, but surely she could retain a degree of control if she didn't give Eli her heart. Her reputation wasn't pristine. Some people would always believe she was a gold-digger. How much more damage could she do by being with Eli Lockwood? Anyway, she was beginning to think he might be a decent guy, despite his old-fashioned tendencies.

"Have dinner with me," he demanded, removing her hand from his stomach. "Any time, any place."

Aria shook her head. She couldn't become involved in that way. Her heart had to stay out of this. "I can't," she said, unsure what had come over her. "I'm sorry. I don't know what I was thinking. I need to cool off."

~

ELI WATCHED ARIA WALK AWAY, her hips swaying and drawing attention to her luscious bottom. Her tanned legs went on for miles. It was a pity she'd turned him down. She'd clearly had second thoughts about backing up her smart mouth. It took a massive amount of willpower to look away. When he did, he noticed other men were watching her, gazing lustfully at her behind and taking advantage of the great view afforded by her tiny bikini. It infuriated Eli. She was here with *him*. These other men needed to drag their minds out of the gutter.

Shit. He had to do something.

She paused to speak to a dark-haired, tattooed surfer with overdeveloped pecs—probably on steroids. The surfer's eyes flicked up and down the length of her body. Anger exploded in Eli's gut, and his grip tightened on his towel, but he stayed where he was. Then Aria smiled at the surfer, and before he was aware of it, Eli had launched himself off the ground and crossed the distance between them. Laying a hand on her shoulder, he swung her around and dragged her body up against his. He ground his lips on hers—hard and demanding. He knew he should be gentle, but she tasted so good. Strawberries and cream. Intoxicating. Her lips parted in surprise, and he slipped his tongue inside her mouth, tasting her more.

He locked eyes with the surfer and was pleased to see him turn away. Then Aria's lips yielded beneath his and she tentatively tasted him back, fingers interlocking at the back of his neck. His arms encircled her waist and pulled her closer. She had to know exactly what she was doing to him. He was afraid the hardness in his shorts would scare her, but instead she pressed closer to him.

They kissed desperately, and Eli knew it had to end, but he couldn't seem to pull away. His entire body was rigid, while she was pliant against him in contrast. He raised a hand and cupped a full and heavy breast.

He wanted her. Had he ever been this hot for someone? Not that he could remember. She moaned into his mouth, and some male part of him roared in triumph. Then she pushed away, and he didn't understand until he saw the dozens of disapproving faces surrounding them. They'd made a spectacle of themselves. Or, more accurately, he'd made a spectacle of them. Again.

"Nothing to see here," he muttered, appalled at his behavior. Damn. Taking Aria's hand in his, he pulled her away from their audience, but not before he'd seen Therese's shocked expression. Double damn.

"What was that about?" Aria demanded once they had more privacy.

Damned if I know. Eli wasn't used to explaining himself. Usually, he had control of every situation, but his attraction to her was slipping wildly out of control.

"I wanted to kiss you," he replied.

"Like that? In front of half of Timaru?"

She looked sexy when she was angry. He itched to pull her back into his arms.

"Don't get me wrong," she continued. "It was amazing. Like, wow. But where did it come from?"

"They were looking at you," he growled, staring at his feet. This couldn't end well. He'd never been jealous over a woman before, but he knew it wasn't a good thing.

"Who?" She was baffled.

"The men," he snapped. "They were all looking at you."

"So, you kissed me because...?"

"Because you're *mine*." The words came out wrong. He knew it as soon as her mouth fell open in surprise. It was the truth, though. Even if he was only now realizing it, she'd been his since he'd kissed her on the porch, and he was going to make her see it somehow. He'd make her change her mind about dating him. "They wanted you. That surfer wanted you. But you're mine."

"Don't I get some say in that?"

"This thing between us... this attraction... I know you feel it too." The way she'd melted into him proved she was as attracted to him as he was to her. "I don't want any other men looking at you, or touching you, or giving you pleasure."

A slow smile worked its way across her features. "You're jealous," she said wonderingly.

"I am not."

"You are." She grinned and traced a finger down his chest. "You want me."

Eli shivered involuntarily beneath her touch. "Of course I want you."

"Eli, those other men don't get to touch me," she said. "And Hemi is only a friend."

"Hemi?"

Her lips quirked. "The surfer. We dated once, but it didn't work out."

The surfer had a name. He was her friend. He'd been with

her before Eli, and chances were, it hadn't been Hemi's decision to end things. "Hemi doesn't feel friendship toward you. I know desire when I see it. He desires you. But you desire me, I know you do."

To prove his point, he slicked an open-mouthed kiss across her lips. "That's the taste of desire, Ri." Then he remembered. He swore, tearing himself away. "Therese is here. We have to get her home."

"Teri is going to a movie tonight with some kids from Itirangi. She's catching a ride back with them."

"You didn't think to clear that with me first?"

"I thought you'd be glad she was making friends."

He would usually have thought her presumptuous, but in this context, it was a blessing in disguise. He grinned like the wolf with Red Riding Hood in his sights. "You're right. This time."

She blinked, bemused.

"Now, there's nothing and nobody to worry about except for you and me."

Understanding dawned. "I have plans tonight," she said.

"Cancel," he ordered. "Say you're not feeling well."

He knew he was pushing his luck, but the thought of her soft, smooth skin rubbing against him was too much to resist. His heart raced as he waited for her reply. He was afraid he'd pushed for too much, too soon.

Finally, Aria leaned up to his ear, a wicked gleam in her eye. "How fast can you get us back to your place?"

CHAPTER 14

*A*s they drove into Itirangi, Aria's bravado wavered. In the face of Eli's jealousy and intensity, going home with him had seemed thrilling, but now she was having second thoughts. When he fumbled with the keys at the front door of his villa, she wondered if it was too late to run. The urge was there, but her attraction to this hunk of a man proved stronger. Yes, she'd probably regret it later, but she wanted this.

When the door swung open, she wondered if the creepy vibe of the house would kill the mood, but Eli's raw sex appeal distracted her. He pinned her against the door as soon as it closed, and they kissed hard and fast, tongues tangling around each other, hands gripping wherever they could.

His kisses started a slow burn between her legs. Aria ran her hands up his firm body. It radiated a heat that made her fingers tingle. She lost herself in the moment, her presence of mind disappearing. Trying to regain some control, she pushed away from the door and backed him against a wall, their mouths glued together. His skin, dry now, felt rough against hers, sending bolts of lust spiraling downwards.

Unable to resist, she slipped her hands inside his shorts and squeezed his butt. Hardened muscle resisted her grasp.

"The bed," Eli panted.

Aria had no idea which room was the master bedroom. She gasped in shock when he swept her feet out from under her, then strode down the hall and deposited her on a large four-poster bed. In seconds, he was on top of her, peeling back her bikini top to expose her breasts. Reverently, he cupped them in his big palms and brushed his thumbs across the nubs. She trembled beneath his ministrations.

"They fit," he murmured. Then he lowered his head and took a breast in his mouth, gently laving and licking, nipping at her.

"Oh, yes," she said on a moan. "That's so good."

She whimpered when he paid the same attention to the other breast and writhed beneath him as he worked his way down her body. He kissed the insides of her thighs, her knees, her calves, then pressed a kiss to the inner arch of each foot before working his way back up again. By the time his mouth closed over her core, Aria was aching to her very soul.

"That's enough!" she cried, overwhelmed by the intensity of the sensations he was creating.

Eli drew back, breathing heavily. His eyes were dark, fixed on her face. There was a question in them, but now wasn't the time for doubts.

"My turn," she said, pushing him back so that he lay beneath her, with his glorious body under her control. She straddled his hips, leaned forward, and kissed him deeply again and again until they were both panting. She slithered downward and kissed his nipples, licking them so they formed hard nubs. Then she kissed his stomach, his thighs. When she took him in her mouth, he twitched against the inside of her cheek. She sucked and licked down his shaft, and he closed his eyes. She stroked his balls, and he groaned.

"Aria." He moaned her name. His fists were clenched at his sides. "No more. Please. If you wanted to torture me, it's working."

She smiled wickedly and bent her head again. Eli gripped her hips and flipped her onto her back, then hovered above her. "Please don't ask me to stop."

"Don't stop," she urged. "Not now."

Eli drove into her up to the hilt. He paused inside her, and she drank in the sensation of being one with him. It was so perfect, so right. Taking his weight onto his forearms, he kissed her, thrusting in and out of her mouth with his tongue, mimicking the actions of their lower bodies. She met him kiss for kiss.

"Mine," he said harshly. "You are *mine*, Aria. No one else's."

She could tell he was holding back, restraining himself. She couldn't have that. She bucked her hips, urging him deeper.

"Say it," he ordered, holding himself above her, frustratingly far away.

She wrapped her legs around his waist. "Take me."

He held back. "Say it."

She opened her eyes. Why was he so far away? Why did this matter to him? "Please, Eli."

"*Say it.*"

She closed her eyes, her head dropped back. "I'm yours."

As if she could ever be anything else. In this moment, he owned her.

"Yes. You are."

Eli thrust into her over and over again. She writhed as the pleasure built within. He moved urgently, and she was with him all the way. His finger slipped between their bodies, and she moaned.

"I can't last much longer," he growled.

"Come," Aria said. "Come now. I'm with you."

His movements became frantic, and Aria crested, pressing against his hard body. The pleasure washed through her, and she cried out at the same moment Eli grunted in release and dropped onto her. She spasmed around him and clenched tightly.

It had never been like this. Never.

She had to do it again.

ARIA WOKE SURROUNDED BY WARMTH. A hairy forearm was resting across her stomach, and a strong chest was pressed against her back. It took a couple of moments to recall where she was, then she couldn't help grinning. Elijah Lockwood was a snuggler. A spooner. How perfectly unlikely.

The smile died on her lips as she realized the enormity of what she'd done.

She'd slept with a powerful man. This would confirm every rumor that had followed her from Christchurch. Everyone would think she'd had sex with him to further her career or her social standing, the same as last time. Unfortunately, this time she was guilty—not of using him, but of the affair, whereas all there had been to her relationship with Wilson Jones was rumor. With Eli, she'd given in to temptation. She'd discredited herself. No one would believe she hadn't slept with Wilson Jones now.

Shit. She had to get out of here.

Wriggling to the edge of the bed, she looked around for her bikini. The top was on the floor, and the bottom was hanging over the lamp. She'd always suspected it would be difficult to extricate herself after casual sex, and this confirmed it. Cheeks hot, mortified, she remembered how uninhibited she'd been—how utterly shameless. At least she was on the pill.

She slid out of Eli's arms, hesitating as he murmured in his sleep, and slipped softly onto her feet. Why did he have to be so adorable? He was sexy as hell when he was awake. It wasn't fair for him to be as cute as a little boy in his sleep. She fetched her bikini and tiptoed out the door, relieved not to have awakened him. She scribbled a quick note, hoping it sounded casual, and jogged to the car. It was only 5 p.m.; there was still time to make it for family dinner. No one needed to know anything.

$\sim$

HE WAS COLD. Why was he cold? He'd gone to bed with a willing woman. Where was she? More importantly, why wasn't she here?

Eli forced his eyes open and patted the bed. The hollow left where Aria had lain was completely cold, which meant she'd been gone for a while. Rolling over, he inhaled the scent of her lingering on the sheets—sweet and fruity. Mingled with the smell of sex, it was intoxicating. *Time for round two.* Sitting up, he looked around. Her clothing was gone. Perhaps she'd gone to make them a drink. Surely she wouldn't leave after something so amazing.

Striding through the house, naked and unashamed, he searched for her. In the kitchen, a piece of notepaper on the bench caught his eye.

Eli

Thanks for the afternoon. It was fun. I'll see you around.

Aria

Eli scrunched the note angrily in his fist. The heat between them had been incredible. The sex, earth-shattering. And she'd dismissed it all as 'fun'? A stab of pain assaulted his senses. For him, it had been so much more than fun, and he wanted to do it again and again and again. He'd thought she felt the same way. His first instinct was to hunt her down, drag her back to bed and torment her in every sensual way he knew until she begged for release. Until she begged for *him*. Just as he'd made her beg this afternoon. The flush on her cheeks when she'd finally capitulated had been perfect.

His libido stirred back to life. Good god, she made him as randy as a teenager.

Usually, he preferred relationships with sophisticated women who understood they were only together temporarily, for mutual satisfaction. It should please him that Aria wouldn't be clingy, but he found himself wishing she'd stayed around for a while longer. Dressing quickly, he made a decision. Their time together wasn't over until he said it was.

ARIA CALLED Sophie as soon as she'd showered and popped dinner in the oven. She recited her story to sounds of disbelief.

"You didn't," Sophie gasped out as soon as she had finished.

"I did," she admitted, shamefaced. "I had crazy sex with Elijah Lockwood."

"That's fantastic!" Sophie squealed.

"No, it's not."

"That's horrible," her friend corrected herself. "Why is it horrible, again?"

"You know what happened in Christchurch," Aria reminded her. "Eli is a far bigger deal than Wilson Jones. What will happen when everyone finds out?"

"You're only human, and he's a babe, Aria. A total sexy beast. No one could hold it against you. And he's not your boss. It's a completely different scenario."

"Last time—"

"Forget last time. Eli isn't Wilson. And you aren't in Christchurch. Everyone here would be happy for you. Hell, I'd be naked in seconds if I thought I had a chance with him."

Oddly, that comforted her.

"Was it good?"

Aria collapsed into an armchair and smiled like a fool. "Better than good. Fireworks."

"I knew it!" Sophie exclaimed. "I'm so jealous."

"You're still separated from Evan?"

"Evan is complicated. I've given him another chance, but I haven't slept with him since we got back together. We're taking it slow."

That was unusual for Sophie, so used to catering to other people's needs.

"Good for you."

"No biggie," her friend said, even though it was. "So, you actually snuck out of bed afterwards?"

"Yeah." Aria winced. "It seemed like the best option at the time."

"You little tramp." Sophie laughed. "Doing the walk of shame."

"It was more like the sprint of shame."

"Will you see him again?"

"Not if I can help it," Aria replied. "I can't handle seeing him. He makes me do stupid things."

"Live a little," Sophie urged. "Be wild. Hot rich guys don't come around too often."

"You're a bad influence, Soph."

"You know you love it."

"Whatever. I've got my family dinner soon. Got to get ready."

"Sure, babes. Make sure to hug those sexy brothers of yours for me."

They hung up, and Aria went to check the pasta bake in the oven. It smelled delicious and would taste even better. Luckily, she still had time to prepare the family dinner and avoid any awkward explanations.

CHAPTER 15

*E*li found Aria's house easily. A quick check of the phone book, and he was on his way. He knew he had the right place when he spotted her ridiculous green Volkswagen parked at the curb along with three other cars. The weatherboard house was painted off-white with pale blue trimmings. Although the garden was weedy, and the grass several centimeters taller than it ought to be, it looked pretty, in an unkempt sort of way. A bird fountain stood beside the porch, and several pairs of shoes were lined up at the door beside a ratty old couch. Perhaps she had friends over. It didn't matter. Eli needed to talk to her.

The door was slightly ajar, but he knocked anyway. A man with unruly black hair and a scruffy beard opened the door, his broad shoulders blocking the doorway so Eli couldn't see inside. As he gave Eli the once-over, the man's upper lip curled into a sneer.

"Who are you?" The question was abrupt to the point of rudeness, but Eli didn't notice; he was too preoccupied with finding out the identity of this man who was in Aria's house, answering her door and looking so damned comfortable about it.

"Eli Lockwood," he said, extending a hand. "And you?"

The man shook his hand with a vice-like grip and glared down his crooked nose. "Justin Simons," he said. "What are you doing here?"

Simons? As in Aria *Simons*? If she was married, it certainly explained why she'd run from his bed. Eli felt a flash of fury. He hated unfaithful women. Now he needed to see her even more urgently.

"I need to see Aria."

"She's busy."

"Can I come in?" Whatever the situation, he wasn't going to be put off. For a moment, he thought he'd have his ass handed to him, but Justin Simons made no move except to lean a forearm casually against the door frame so he loomed over Eli.

"What's this about?"

"That's between Aria and me."

"Humor me," Justin said. "Or you can bloody well piss off."

"It's work-related."

Justin watched him, suspicion radiating from every one of his pores, but backed off and stepped aside to let Eli in. The door opened directly into the kitchen, which was in absolute chaos. An older couple was sitting at the table, playing a spirited card game while a solidly built guy fried half a dozen steaks on an indoor barbeque. Aria was tossing meals on plates, and food was strewn across the available counter space. The tall, dark-haired girl he'd seen her with at Davy's Bar was pouring alcohol and juice into a punch bowl with no apparent formula.

Justin closed the door behind him and said, "Are you sure you don't want to come back tomorrow?"

Eli took a deep breath and nodded.

"Aria!" Justin called. "You've got a guest."

Guest. If Eli was a guest, then what were all these other

people? Surely they didn't live here. Aria spun around, her wild curls bouncing around her ears, and Eli pictured that hair fanned out across the pillows as he pushed into her. There was a stirring in his pants. *Think unsexy thoughts.*

"Eli, what are you doing here?" Her friendly smile was fixed in place, but the warmth faded from her eyes.

"I could ask you the same thing. I can see it's not a good time."

"Nonsense," the older woman said as she struggled to shuffle the deck of cards, her fingers too short to do a good job of it. Plump, with cropped auburn hair and rosy cheeks, she smiled at him welcomingly, the only person in this madhouse who had done so. "Have a seat. We're almost ready to eat."

That's right. He'd forgotten about her family dinner.

"Why don't you introduce us?" Justin suggested.

She looked flustered but recovered quickly. "Of course. This is my mum and dad, Donna and Geoff." She gestured to the couple playing cards. "My friend Avery." The tall girl with the deep-set eyes. "And my brothers, Cooper and Justin."

Her brothers. Thank freaking God. Eli studied the two men. There was a certain degree of resemblance—both brothers and Aria had olive complexions—but the men dwarfed her.

"Family, this is Elijah Lockwood."

"Of Lockwood Holdings?" the tall girl, Avery, asked. Her voice was slightly husky, like she smoked. While she resembled the girls Eli usually dated, she didn't appeal to him at all. Her model-like figure couldn't compare to Aria, who was earthy and sexy and a little bit fun.

"Yes," he said quickly, to cover the moment of awkwardness. Avery glanced at Aria, and he could have sworn his lover shrank a couple of inches.

"How interesting to see you here," Avery said. "I didn't realize you and Aria were friends."

She was astute, this woman.

"We're acquaintances," Aria cut in. "I'm interviewing him for an article, but it can wait until Monday. Mr. Lockwood is just overeager." As neatly as that, she'd managed to direct him to the door.

Was she embarrassed by him? He hadn't considered the possibility, and it made him uncomfortable. Women had always been proud to take him home.

"Your company has bought the balance lot of the subdivision on the hill, right?" Cooper Simons asked without turning away from the barbeque. "Lakeview?"

"That's right." He sensed the mood in the room shift and wondered if perhaps he shouldn't have been so honest.

"You're making life difficult for a lot of people," Justin said.

"I don't mean anyone any harm," Eli replied cautiously. "It's business."

"For some people, poor business means no food on the table," Justin retorted.

"Oh, hush up," Aria's mother ordered, rolling her eyes. "I'm sorry, Elijah. My son fancies a florist who will be facing competition from your new mall. That's why he's being such a grouch."

"Emily will be all right," Avery said. "She's clever and talented. Plenty of people will still buy from her."

"We'll see," Justin grumbled, his cheeks flaming red.

"How long have you known our Aria?" Cooper asked, nimbly changing the subject.

"Just for a few days," Eli replied, grateful for a respite from the questions about his business but wary of Cooper's scrutiny as well. The other man didn't seem as blatantly hostile as his brother, but experience had taught Eli that that didn't mean much.

Cooper turned to Aria. "Say, what were you up to today, Ri? Heard from Hemi he saw you at the beach in Timaru."

113

"Yeah," she replied cautiously, begging Eli with her eyes not to give her up. "I was there with a girlfriend."

"That's funny." Cooper grinned, his smile reminding Eli of a cat toying with a mouse. "Hemi said you were with a man."

"My friend's brother," she said quickly.

Eli watched the interchange with interest, noting that Cooper's gaze slid from him to Aria and back.

"You kiss all your friends' brothers, Ri? Or just the lucky ones?"

Donna gasped and dropped the pack of cards. "You went on a date today? Why didn't you tell us, darling? Who was it with? How did it go?"

Eli smiled despite himself. Aria pinned him with a look. If looks could kill...

"It went badly, Mum," she muttered through gritted teeth. "That's why I didn't mention it."

"Oh, but I'm so glad to hear you're putting yourself out there again. It's been long enough." Apparently, Eli wasn't the only one having a dry spell. At least he didn't have to deal with his family pushing him to get back into the dating game. "I never understood why you broke up with that lovely Hemi," Donna continued.

"We didn't suit, Mum."

Eli had the feeling they'd had similar conversations many times before. He cleared his throat. Donna glanced up.

"Sorry, Elijah!" she exclaimed. "I forgot you were there. Won't you eat with us?"

"Yes," Aria said defeatedly, looking from her mother to her brother to Eli and finally at the floor. "Why don't you join us?"

Eli couldn't help but enjoy Aria's discomfort. She deserved it for disappearing from his bed. He took a seat at the edge of the table, and as if by some miracle, a dinner appeared before him from the mess on the counter, along with a glass of fizzy orange punch.

The hearty steak and pasta bake smelled delicious, and the banter during dinner was light-hearted and teasing. They ignored him for the most part, except for a few suspicious glances from Justin, assessing looks from Cooper, and shrewd questions from Avery. Although she stopped asking questions eventually, he got the feeling she suspected things weren't as they appeared. Maybe Aria wasn't the sort of person to bring work home on the weekends, or maybe he reeked of dishonesty.

While Donna cleared the dishes away, Aria laid a hand on his shoulder and drew him into the bathroom, closing the door behind them.

"What game are you playing?" she demanded.

In response, he gripped her hips and claimed her lips in a hot, hungry kiss—something he'd been aching to do since he woke to find an empty bed. At first she resisted, but within seconds she was sinking into him, winding her arms around his neck and surrendering sweetly to his onslaught.

Eli broke free, feeling triumphant. "I knew it!"

Her eyes were still hazed with passion, and she squeezed them shut. "What?"

"You still want me. What we have between us isn't over."

Aria swallowed. "It has to be over because it should never have happened."

"Why not?" He bent and took her mouth in another kiss, slow and drugging. "We're good together."

"We—we—uh..."

"Yes?" he taunted when she couldn't string a sentence together. "You started this, Aria, when you turned up in my living room at the crack of dawn, looking like a damned angel. But I decide when it's finished."

"We're too different," she said. "I shouldn't have given in to the attraction. It was a mistake."

"Too late for that, sweetheart," he countered.

"Damn, you're frustrating," she snapped.

"Sexually?" His eyes glittered with humor. "Can you resist?"

There was a flash of doubt in her eyes, but she replied firmly, "No to the first, yes to the second."

Then she brushed past him and went back to her guests.

AVERY LINGERED after Aria had shooed everyone else out. When they were sitting alone with a bottle of Irish whiskey, she said, "Well, that was interesting."

"I don't know what you mean," Aria replied.

Avery scoffed. "Don't play dumb. There was practically a high-voltage cable between you and Eli Lockwood."

"Okay," Aria relented. "He's gorgeous. I'm not blind."

"It's more than that," Avery insisted. "Something happened between the two of you."

"How could you possibly know that?"

"Give me a little credit, Ri. You were blushing like a schoolgirl all night."

"We made love," she admitted.

"Whoa."

"What?" Aria asked. "You said you could tell."

"I could tell something had happened, but I didn't realize you'd gone that far."

"It's not a big deal, is it?" People had one-night stands all the time. Not her, sure. But others. It was the twenty-first century, for crying out loud.

"For you, it's huge."

"What do you mean 'for me'?" There was an insult attached to that comment; she was sure of it.

"You're a great friend, Ri. You know that. But you're emotionally challenged when it comes to men."

Ouch. Okay, perhaps Avery was right, but it wasn't relevant. Eli wasn't her boyfriend, nor did she want him to be. Those knee-knocking kisses were fantastic, but she wasn't going down that road again.

She. Was. *Not*. Interested.

"It's not a big deal," she reiterated. "It was a once-off."

One that she'd regretted a hundred different ways already tonight.

"It's too bad," Avery remarked.

"What's too bad?"

"I wouldn't mind getting sweaty with your Elijah, but it's never going to happen."

Aria felt a twinge of jealousy. Why should it matter to her that Avery found Eli attractive? "Why not?"

"He's only interested in you. Duh."

Aria grinned, feeling quite satisfied with herself. Then she realized she'd played right into Avery's hands. Oh, no. What was she going to do with herself?

CHAPTER 16

*E*arly Monday afternoon, Aria knocked on the Lockwoods' door. She couldn't believe she was here, but she *had* made a promise to help Teri. It wouldn't be fair if she abandoned that promise because she'd crossed a boundary with Eli.

"Teri!" she called when no one answered the door. "You in there?"

Teri opened the door and looked at her warily. "What are you doing here?"

She supposed she deserved the censure after what Teri had witnessed at the beach. As a woman with two older brothers, she knew no girl wanted to see their brother necking. In public, no less.

"I was hoping to see you," she replied. She was also praying Eli was not at home. His development had been approved by the council that morning, so she assumed he would be at the work site, supervising the contractors while they got started. "I wanted to know how your date went the other night."

"Oh." Teri looked younger today, the dark makeup absent

from under her eyes. "That's cool. You want to come in? You can see the kitten. I've got him for a little while longer yet."

"I'd love to." She really would. Part of her was relieved at how easily Teri had let her in. She had been worried she'd be turned away without a word. "How is the kitty?"

"He's great," Teri said with a grin. "I love him."

Her enthusiasm was contagious. Aria had been concerned that the novelty would wear off quickly; now she was concerned that Teri might get too attached to the kitten. This was only temporary, after all.

Teri led her into one of the bedrooms. It had unadorned, whitewashed walls, and the open cupboards were free of clutter except for a makeup bag on the bedside table. Someone had vacuumed the floor recently, and the dirty washing sat tidily in a basket in the corner. It was bizarre. When Aria was a teenage girl, boy band posters had plastered the walls of her bedroom, and stacks of books and knick-knacks had rendered her cupboards invisible. Even though this was only Teri's home for a short while, the lack of color in the room saddened Aria. Teri might be rich, but she'd clearly missed out on the chaos of normal childhood.

"Here he is." Teri grabbed a purring ball of fur from the bed and held him out.

Taking him in one hand so she could pat him with the other, Aria said, "What a cutie."

"Totally."

They both fell silent for a moment.

"So, um," Teri began awkwardly. "About you and Eli..."

Aria closed her eyes, shoving the memory of their passionate embrace on the beach, and what had followed, to the back of her mind. "Nothing is going on between us," she said. "We got carried away, that's all."

"Looked like a bit more than that," Teri muttered. She stared at her feet, her forehead creased. "I like you," she said eventually. "But Eli's girlfriends are usually bitches. I don't want you to be like that."

It broke Aria's heart how serious she was, and how much thought she must have put into this.

"I promise not to be a bitch," Aria said. "And I'll be your friend for as long as you want me to." It shouldn't be a difficult promise to keep. Teri was special, and before long, she'd be living in the North Island, having completely forgotten about the nobody reporter from Itirangi. "Now, tell me about the cute boy from the beach," Aria ordered. Teri giggled, and the sound of her laughter lifted Aria's mood. "Tell me *all* about it."

RETURNING HOME to the sound of female laughter was a new experience. Eli paused at the door, straining to hear the lowered voices over the pounding of his heart. One was Therese. The other made him hesitate for a beat longer than usual. It was Aria; he was almost certain of it. But what was she doing here?

Although he had no intention of leaving her alone as she'd requested, he assumed he'd need to be persuasive if he wanted her back in his bed. Yet here she was, laughing with his sister, a miracle in itself. Therese had barely spoken to him since Saturday. Funny how she seemed to have no problem talking to Aria. Was there some sort of female club he was excluded from, whose mission in life was to baffle unsuspecting men? It seemed likely. The alternative, that Eli was terrible at communicating with his sister, was another likely scenario. His empathy with children left a lot to be desired, but it was irrelevant because he never planned to have any of his own. No child deserved to be subjected to the sort of cold upbringing he'd endured. Eli was confident that in deciding not to have children, he was making a more responsible choice than his parents had.

Moving quietly, he made his way to Therese's door and peeked inside, his breath catching. His sister was sitting cross-legged on the bed, relaying a story with animated gestures. Aria was smiling and nodding, encouraging her while she patted the kitten sprawled across her lap. The scene was so sweet, he couldn't help but watch. Therese was mid-sentence.

"...thought the movie was great, but I didn't love it. He held my hand the whole time, though, and that, like, totally made up for it. He's so cute. I'm so happy my first date wasn't a total flop," she gushed. "It was great. But I suppose you've been on heaps of dates."

Now, things were getting interesting. Eli leaned forward, straining to hear Aria's answer.

"I've been on my fair share," she replied, annoyingly vague. "Nothing wonderful, though. The best was a ballet show. I'm not a huge fan of ballet, but there's something romantic about going to see a live performance."

"What would your dream date be?" Therese asked.

"A beach," Aria said without hesitation. "Imagine getting whisked away to a tropical island for a weekend. You could go for a horse trek down the beach and finish with a picnic."

Therese sighed. "My parents could afford that a million times over, but they'd never spend their money that way."

Eli heard the truth in her words and felt for her. It was the first time he'd understood his sister's position. Being a Lockwood was lonely and often disheartening. Feeling guilty for eavesdropping, he rapped on the door.

"Come in," Therese called. When he did, her nose crinkled up. "You look gross."

Just great. Aria looked fresh and lovely in a pair of baby-blue shorts and a high-necked shirt, while he looked 'gross'.

"I probably smell worse," he admitted.

"Hi," Aria said softly, chewing on her lower lip. "I thought you'd be working."

That explained a few things. She hadn't intended to see him. In fact, she'd probably come in the middle of the day to avoid him.

He shrugged. "I came home for lunch and a quick run. Why are you here?"

"To see Teri," she replied, stroking the kitten's stomach.

His sister must have picked up on the tension in the room. "Talk properly," she said. "I can't handle your weird silent conversation."

"We don't need to talk," Aria replied at the same time Eli said, "Yes, let's talk."

Teri looked from one to the other and raised an eyebrow. "If you're going to talk, you'd better do it out there." She pointed at the door. "This is *my* bedroom, you know."

Aria looked as if she was considering making a run for it through the open window.

"Please talk to me," he said.

"Fine," she agreed, then handed the kitten to Teri and tried to smooth the fur off her shorts.

When they were in the hall, Aria looked him up and down. "How about you have a shower, and we'll talk afterwards?"

Was he that bad? Eli surreptitiously sniffed his armpit. Yup, he was that bad. "Give me ten minutes."

ARIA'S MOUTH had gone dry when Eli walked into the room, breathtakingly sexy in running shorts and a singlet. Her brain had gone blank, so she'd done the smart thing and pretended to be disgusted by him. When he came back nine and a half minutes later (she'd timed it), she focused on her chipped fingernails rather than admire the way his damp hair curled against his shoulders.

"What did you want to talk about?" she asked, taking a direct approach.

"Us." The word was clipped.

"There is no us," she said. If she wanted him to leave her alone before she lost her dignity and her heart, she needed to push him away. "We made a mistake. I got carried away. I shouldn't have let it happen, and it won't happen again."

"Nice try," he said, taking a few steps toward her. There was a hint of swagger in his steps, as if he was confident he would win their standoff. "But I'm onto you, princess. You want me."

Another step forward, and his chest brushed hers. Aria's hand came up to rest over his heart. She'd been planning to shove him away, but, instead, her fingers fisted the fabric of his shirt, drawing him closer. Maybe it was time to be honest.

"I want you, Eli," she confessed. "But I don't *want* to want you."

"That doesn't make any sense," he said, resting his palm across the back of her neck. Involuntarily, she leaned into his touch. He took her movement as encouragement and lowered his lips to hers.

The moment they touched, Aria sprang away. "You can't kiss me."

He looked bemused. "I just did."

She stomped her foot, feeling ridiculous, but she needed to make a statement. "You're not listening to me."

"You're not making sense," he teased, cupping a hand under her chin.

She jerked out of his grip. "If you can't respect my choices, then I can't have you in my life."

Finally, he seemed to realize how serious she was, and the smile faded from his face.

"I see." He was already distancing himself from her, closing himself off, even though he hadn't moved. It was what she'd asked for, but that didn't stop the twinge of disappointment.

Eli didn't say anything else, and she didn't explain. She couldn't tell him how messed up she was about men when she didn't fully understand it herself. As she walked away, her footfalls echoed throughout the house, and the click of the front door was loud in the unnatural silence.

~

ELI STARED AT THE DOOR. Nothing was going the way he wanted. He'd known his beautiful Aria desired him, and he'd thought he could sway her around to his way of thinking, as he so often did with business acquaintances, but he'd miscalculated. There was more to this than met the eye. He needed help.

Only one person he knew never put a foot wrong with women, and that was Mark Talbot. The prominent lawyer was a playboy of the first degree. He'd dated scores of women and had a reputation for loving them and leaving them. More impressive was the fact that ninety-nine percent of the time, he parted amicably from his paramours.

Eli dialed Mark's number three times before Mark picked up.

"This had better be good," his friend said good-naturedly. "I have company."

"I need help," Eli said, getting straight to the point.

"Are we talking legal help, or 'I killed my neighbor and I want to bury the body' help? Because my company is very lovely and very naked."

"I need help with a woman."

"Then you've come to the right person."

Eli could hear the grin in Mark's voice. "Is it worth your time?"

"Buddy, hearing you ask for help is *always* worth my time. If it's about a woman, then all the better. I've never known you to be at a loss with a girl. Just give me a moment." Muffled noises sounded on the other end of the phone. "The lovely Elouise is standing by to give her opinion as well. What's the situation?"

"I think I've upset this woman," Eli began. "We slept together, and now she doesn't want to know me."

Mark laughed. "Was it that bad for her, then?"

Eli scowled. "There were no complaints at the time." It had been indescribably good for him. Surely, it had been the same for her too. While she might say she didn't want him, her body sent a very different message. Lack of chemistry certainly wasn't the problem.

"Tell me about her."

How best to describe her? He didn't want to outright admit to Mark that he'd been correct in assuming Eli was interested in Aria for more than her connection with Teri. "She's bossy and sweet and quirky," he said.

"Interesting. What does she do for a living?"

Busted. "She's a journalist."

"Ah, the reporter you asked me to look into. I thought as much. I have the information you requested."

"Thanks," Eli said, wondering if his friend had found anything.

"She's pretty," Mark added.

"She's *mine*," Eli snapped. He couldn't help it. Even if no one else realized it yet, and even if only for a short time, she was his. Pity she was the type who would want children. If he thought she'd be happy remaining childless forever, then he

125

could imagine spending his life with her. She was unusual and passionate, and she'd be able to keep him on his toes. Unfortunately, she seemed to have those pesky maternal instincts, which made her perfect for helping with Teri but totally unsuitable for being his partner. He and Aria would have to go their separate ways at some point, but he wasn't ready for it to happen yet.

"Of course," Mark murmured. "Do you know what I found?"

"Probably not much," Eli guessed. "She seems like a straight arrow."

"Not quite."

The tone of Mark's voice made him uneasy. "What did you find?"

"Your lady friend worked at the *Press* in Christchurch until a year ago, when rumor has it she slept with the boss to get a promotion."

Eli shook his head emphatically, forgetting Mark couldn't see him. "I don't believe it."

"The co-worker I spoke to was convinced of it."

It couldn't be true. Aria wasn't the type. "That's not the woman I know."

"It might not be who she is now, but I'm telling you that's who she was. Are you sure this girl isn't using you?"

Eli stopped to think about it. What would Aria gain by sleeping with him, then pushing him away? Nothing. And besides, what they had between them was too special. It couldn't be fake. "She's not."

"If you say so." Mark clearly didn't believe it. "Tell me more about her."

Eli shook his head, trying to erase the accusation against Aria from his mind. "She has two brothers."

"Uh-oh."

"What?" Eli was tired of Mark's cryptic statements.

"If you upset her and she goes running to her brothers,

they'll want to destroy you." Mark was far too pleased by the prospect. "Are they big guys?"

Eli gulped. "Bigger than me."

"Avoid girls with brothers. It's just asking for trouble. She's a hometown girl?"

"Yeah. She grew up here, although she must have lived somewhere else while she earned her degree."

"She's an educated woman," Mark commented. "Interesting."

"I date educated women," Eli interjected, taking issue with his friend's tone.

"You date women who speak multiple languages and were born into power and influence, not necessarily ones who have gone out of their way to earn an education."

What was the difference?

"Elouise agrees with me. She's studying for a diploma in interior design, isn't that right, sweetums?" A murmur in the background. "The point is, winning over this girl of yours requires different techniques from the ones you usually use. What did you do to upset her?"

"I don't know."

"Then don't try to figure it out. It'll hurt your brain. Women aren't logical, Eli. Their instincts aren't logical. Now, what does she want?"

"My head on a platter? For aliens to probe me?"

Mark chuckled. "Realistically, what does she want from you?"

"She wants me to leave her alone. She wants a good story." Realization struck. "She wants to be accepted and respected by her town. She loves this little backwater."

Mark was quiet while the cogs turned in his brain. "Clearly, option one is out. Option two as well, unless you've changed your view on making a fool of yourself in the media. Option three, we can work with. She loves her town. How can you use that knowledge to impress her?"

Eli couldn't say, off the top of his head, but Mark had given him a lot to think about. "Appreciate your help," he said. "It was good talking to you." Then he hung up and started brainstorming possibilities. Before long, he struck gold. His plan wouldn't be quick to put into action, but it would be effective.

CHAPTER 17

*B*efore long, Aria turned her attention to other work. She looked for stories that didn't involve Elijah Lockwood or Lockwood Holdings Limited. There were few. She wrote an article about the 100th anniversary of the local fire brigade, and one about the local kid who'd been awarded a rugby scholarship, then her editor directed her to write a series of articles following the construction of the mall complex. The editor was certain that Aria was the best person for the job, considering her background knowledge about the development. Aria couldn't convince her otherwise, but by interviewing the architect, the interior designer and the draughtsman, she did manage to produce three articles without needing to contact Eli. A good effort.

She also wrote a human interest story about the whirlwind romance between the architect and the interior designer, whom had found they shared more than a passion for design. Aria envied them. When they looked into each other's eyes, it was as if she wasn't even in the room. She wanted a love like that more than anything.

Sometimes, she found herself thinking about Eli and the potential she saw in him. If only he were an everyday guy——

a teacher, a farmer or a mechanic——then maybe she would be able to pursue a relationship with him. But no, he was the millionaire owner of a nationwide property development company, the sort of guy who would never be compatible with her and who could ruin her with only a couple of phone calls if he chose to. Unfortunately, no matter how many times she reminded herself why she avoided powerful men, she couldn't help but remember how vulnerable he'd been in his relationship with Teri, and how willing he'd been to open himself to new things to make her happy. But it didn't matter. He wasn't part of her life anymore. The foundations were ready to be laid for his mall, and she was no longer involved.

～

FOUR WEEKS to the day after issuing his challenge, Derek summoned Aria and Johnny Chen into his office. Unlike last time, when she'd been fidgety and nervous, Aria felt surprisingly calm as she stood before Derek's solid desk like a criminal in front of a jury. She'd done the best she could while keeping her integrity intact. She was proud of herself, and she couldn't ask for more than that. If Johnny Chen had outdone her, so be it. She'd intentionally avoided the sports columns for the past month so she wouldn't be tempted to draw comparisons.

"Mr. Chen, Miss Simons," Derek said after his customary delay. "Welcome. The other editors and I have been very pleased with your efforts over the past four weeks. You've both produced excellent work, even in the absence of any significant newsworthy events."

Aria stood tall and kept her gaze straight. Johnny shifted next to her. She wished there could be a promotion for both of them. He was a nice guy, but senior positions didn't grow on trees.

"The reporter who has impressed us most, is, by a hair, Miss Simons."

Aria's head spun, and she thought she might faint. She stayed upright by the power of inertia, and nothing else.

"Congratulations, Miss Simons. You are the *South Canterbury Chronicle*'s new Senior Reporter."

"Thank you so much," she said, pressing her palms together. Her eyes welled up, but she blinked the tears back. *Don't be ridiculous.* Turning to Johnny, she gave him a swift hug. "I'm sorry you missed out."

"Don't be," he said, clapping her back despite his obvious disappointment. "You deserved it."

Finally hearing this from someone else's lips, she could have cried. His words meant more to her than the promotion. More to her than anything.

She had her pride back.

~

A FEW WEEKS LATER, Aria had mastered the art of evasion, and hadn't seen or spoken to Eli since she'd stormed out of his house. She tried to comfort herself with her new promotion and tell herself that the distance was what she needed, but she desperately wanted to see him again. She wasn't moping, exactly, but she wasn't her usual cheerful self, and her friends and family had noticed.

Justin had offered to give Eli a black eye, and Sophie had suggested they drown their sorrows together, but Aria hadn't taken either of them up on their offer. Quiet time was what she needed. She busied herself writing about neighborhood disputes, baked over a dozen cakes and watched endless reruns of *Friends*.

On top of her being in a funk, something was conspicuously missing: her monthly. Usually, she was as regular as clockwork—as punctual in her cycle as everything else—but now there was no sign of it. Her breasts were tender, and meals were difficult to keep down. She hadn't told anyone. Hadn't even done a test. She was too afraid.

Aria's plan for her personal life had been as follows: find a nice guy, get married, have babies. Two, preferably, but she'd be happy with any. By the time a baby arrived, she'd be a few years older, with more to offer, and a husband on the scene. Having a baby now didn't fit into her plan. She was single and only finding her footing. Although her family would always stand by her, it wasn't the same as having a partner.

Even though she hadn't taken the test yet, she was certain of the result. She was pregnant. She'd never missed a period before, and she'd had unprotected sex. It all added up. She was on the pill, but occasionally she forgot to take it because she never actually expected to have sex. She'd been in an eighteen-month dry spell, after all. Her carelessness had landed her in this predicament.

Aria purchased a pregnancy test using the self-checkout option at a supermarket in Timaru—knowing that if she bought one in Itirangi, the entire town would know inside of an hour, including her brothers, her parents and her friends. She'd rather delay telling them for as long as possible. It was humiliating. How had she been so irresponsible?

Within a minute of dipping it, two pink lines appeared on the stick. Positive. Although it wasn't a surprise, the lines took her breath away. Closing her eyes, she leaned back against the toilet cistern and breathed deeply.

It's all right. A wave of nausea roiled her stomach. *Don't panic. You wanted a baby eventually, right? It's just coming earlier than you expected.*

A few tears trickled down her cheeks, and she sniffled. She had to tell Eli. But how? She'd been so harsh last time she'd spoken to him. How would he react to the news?

He'll want to be involved, she reassured herself. He might be hesitant around children, but he would learn. Unfortunately, she'd be a burden on him for the rest of his life. How perfectly awful. Aria was sick of being a burden on people. It had taken a lot for her to swallow her pride when she'd turned up on her parents' doorstep late at night with a suitcase in hand and nowhere to go, having left the *Press* behind. She'd been doing so well since then. Why had she been so stupid? And why did life have to be so damn difficult?

~

ELI'S SEPARATION from Aria was slow torture as time crawled by. He was working on his plan to win her back, but it was taking longer than he expected, and he was losing enthusiasm for it. Teri sympathized with him, and even hugged him before she boarded a flight back to Auckland. Although he hadn't seen Aria in weeks, Teri had. The two of them had visited the beach again and gone walking behind the lake a couple of times, but when he asked about Aria, Teri refused to answer any of his questions.

His daily visits to the construction site were the only times he left the house, and even there, he was no longer needed. To be honest, there was no longer any need for him to remain in Itirangi. Things were going smoothly. But, although he knew he should return to Auckland, he couldn't bring himself to leave. He liked Itirangi—liked waking up to fresh air and the sound of birds rather than traffic. Most of all, he wanted to see Aria once more before he left.

Eli was sitting at the dining table in his rented villa, studying architectural plans on his laptop, when there was a knock on the door. He strode down the hallway and was flabbergasted to find Aria on his porch. He blinked at her. She was a vision in a purple sundress, hair curling over her shoulders and a pair of chunky blue heels on her feet. His pulse stuttered. She was more beautiful than he remembered, and he ached to touch her, but the hurt from her rejection still felt raw.

"Good morning, Eli," she said softly, a hesitant smile on her lips. Despite the smile, her knuckles, where she was clutching her purse, were white, and her expression was strained.

"I wasn't expecting you," he murmured. "What are you doing here?"

The question wasn't meant to be harsh, but she flinched nonetheless.

"I'm sorry," he said. "I'll start again. Good morning, Aria. How are you?"

"I've been better," she replied, studying her toes. "We need to talk."

Those four words were enough to terrify any sane male. "What is it?"

"Can I come in?"

She sounded unsure of herself, and he wondered what could be sapping her confidence. When he looked closer, he noticed dark circles under her eyes and splotchy cheeks. Had she been sleeping poorly?

"Sure." Holding the door open, he stepped back to let her through. The house was in disarray, but if she'd expected something different, then that was too bad. They sat at the table, and he pushed his laptop to the side. "All right, you're worrying me," he said gently as she lowered herself into a chair. "Do you want to tell me why you're here?"

"Eli..."

She gazed at his face wistfully, and he wanted to grab her and kiss her until she surrendered. The next words out of her mouth stopped him dead.

"I'm pregnant."

What? But how? He didn't understand. He'd heard the words, but they made no sense. *Pregnant... Pregnant... I'm pregnant...*

"Uh, what?" He sounded dumb, even to his own ears.

"Eli." She reached across the table and took his hand in hers. "When we made love, we didn't use a condom. I'm pregnant."

Slowly, it started to sink in. She was pregnant. With his baby. Or was she? He thought of his ex-girlfriends, other girls who had wanted to trap him into marriage. Women could be devious creatures. What had Mark said? Aria had slept her way to a promotion. She wasn't afraid to use sex to get what she wanted.

"Are you sure it's mine? Or did you plan this?"

"How can you even ask that?" she demanded. "I haven't been with anyone else. I want a baby, but not yet, and not like this."

He regretted the questions immediately. Of course the baby was his. She wasn't the sort of girl to sleep around. If she had been, she would've come back to his bed when he'd asked.

"Are you sure you're pregnant?" he asked, clutching at straws.

"I'm several weeks late," she said. "I'm getting morning sickness. I took a test. I'm sure."

"Oh."

"I know this is a lot to process," she said, wringing her hands.

"Didn't you say you were on the pill?" He was sure she had at some point. He never would have gone without protection otherwise.

"It isn't one hundred percent effective," she explained. "And I'm not as careful as I should be because it's been so long since I've been with anybody."

"We're having a baby."

He was in shock. That was the only explanation. He couldn't think properly. His brain was fuzzy, and all he could focus on was that one thought: *I'm going to be a dad*. Eli wasn't ready to be a dad. He hadn't planned to be a dad, and he certainly wasn't cut out for it. He was too similar to his parents. His child would be doomed to a lifetime without fatherly affection.

Eli's gaze rested on her stomach. It was still flat, but his child was growing inside her. "Can I...?"

Aria nodded. He crossed to her and pressed his hands to her stomach.

"I can't believe it," he said. "We're having a baby."

"I'm sorry," she apologized, looking utterly miserable. "I should have been more careful. I was so stupid."

"It's not your fault," Eli told her, running his hands over her warm skin. "I should have used a condom, just to be safe."

Aria finally met his eyes. "You're not mad?"

"I wouldn't have wanted this to happen, but I'm not mad at you," he said honestly. "Don't blame yourself. You're no more responsible for this than I am. I'll support you completely. Anything you need, just ask. I'll contribute my share."

"Your share? This isn't a cake, Eli. It's a baby. We need to work together to do the best we can."

He frowned. "I'm happy to support you and the baby, but I can't be part of its life. I can't be an active parent. You have no idea what my childhood was like. I'm not deluded enough to think I could do a better job than my parents did."

Drawing away from him, Aria raised her chin defiantly and sniffled, tears glistening in her eyes. "You would rather your child not know its father? A loving family is important. Our son or daughter needs both parents."

She was so caring, his Aria. So warm and loving. Their child would never lack affection with her as a mother. "I have every faith in you, sweetheart. You'll be a wonderful mother. The baby won't need me. In fact, it will be better off without me around to complicate things."

She swayed on her feet, and he wrapped his arms around

her, resisting her attempts to shake him off. Finally, she settled against his chest and let the tears fall, wetting his shirt.

"I'm so scared," she whispered.

It felt right to have her back in his arms, no matter what the circumstances. If that made him messed up, then so be it. They were bound to each other now. Possessiveness surged through him so strongly that it frightened him. He had no right to Aria. No right to her body. But he wanted to hold her close and give her what little comfort he could.

"It's going to be fine," he promised. After all, with his money and a mother's love, their baby would be well taken care of.

CHAPTER 18

*A*ria left once she'd pulled herself back together. Eli had taken the news far better than she'd hoped, but his insistence on being a distant figure in their child's life concerned her. Maybe he needed time to process the news and adjust to the idea of being a father before they discussed particulars.

Aria still hadn't told her parents and had no idea how to go about it. People had sex outside of marriage all the time, but most casual encounters didn't result in pregnancy, so most people didn't have to confess to their parents about it.

An even more horrifying thought occurred to her. How would Eli's parents take the news? They'd probably assume she'd become pregnant to trap him, when nothing could be further from the truth. In an ideal situation, she'd raise the baby herself without accepting anyone's charity, but although she could stretch her budget to cover a baby, she wouldn't be able to work full-time once it was born. She might as well flush her promotion down the drain, for all the good it would do her now. She needed help.

Eli's reticence disappointed her. She'd hoped he would be an equal partner in parenthood. Although he might not believe it, he would be a good dad. And while it would be difficult for her to have him around but not taste his kisses or feel him against her, it would be the best thing for the baby.

Their baby.

The idea was starting to grow on her. It wasn't like she had any choice in the matter, so she might as well embrace it.

Over the weekend, she picked up some baby-related items in Timaru, where fewer people would recognize her, and then conference-called Sophie and Avery.

When they answered, she didn't bother with the usual formalities. "Come to my place."

"What's wrong?" Sophie asked.

"Nothing," Aria replied quickly. "Well, I guess something, but it's also exciting. If you don't come, you'll be disappointed later."

"Give me ten minutes," Avery said before hanging up abruptly.

"Polite as always," Sophie muttered sarcastically. "I'll be there soon, babes."

ARIA LUGGED the bags into her living room. She poured two glasses of wine and one of sparkling grape juice, then opened a packet of Tim-Tams, a rare indulgence, and popped one into her mouth.

Sophie arrived before Avery. She must have jumped into her car as soon as she got off the phone because she was wearing sweatpants, a baggy singlet and fluffy slippers. Avery arrived only a few minutes later, looking far more composed. Aria handed them each a glass of wine and sipped her own drink while they got comfortable on the couch.

"Are you going to tell us what happened?" Sophie asked, eyes bright with excitement.

Aria tilted her head toward the shopping bags in the

139

corner of the room, and they followed her gaze. Most were tied shut, and it was impossible to tell what was inside them, but a teddy bear was peeking out the top of one bag, and a bassinet stood behind them.

"Holy shit," Avery breathed, her eyes darting from the bags to Aria and back again. "Are you saying what I think you're saying?"

Aria rubbed a hand over her belly and nodded. "I'm pregnant."

"Oh. My. God." Sophie was gobsmacked. Her eyes widened, her jaw dropped, and she squealed. "Wow! You're having a baby! I'm going to be an aunty." She froze, her grin fixed. "Wait. Is this something we're excited about, or something we're horrified about?"

Aria shrugged. "I was horrified at first, but I'm excited now. A bit scared. Make that terrified. I don't know how to be a mum." Wasn't that the truth? But she had the best role model. If she could emulate her mother, she'd be great.

Sophie squealed again, and Avery looked at her in disgust. "Get hold of yourself."

"I always knew you'd be first!" Sophie cried, engulfing Aria in a surprisingly tight hug, considering her slight frame. Aria and Avery exchanged glances. They'd always expected Sophie to be the first to get pregnant.

"Are you calling me a loose woman?" Aria asked teasingly.

"Yeah, right," Sophie scoffed. "You love kids, babe. It makes sense you'd want one before the rest of us."

"Three guesses who the father is," Avery remarked.

Sophie hugged her again. "It's Eli Lockwood, isn't it?"

Aria nodded. With all she'd been doing, she'd forgotten his involvement for a few hours, but now she remembered the way he'd held her when she'd told him she was pregnant. Tears welled up, and she willed them to stay where they were.

"Aww, honey," Sophie soothed, rubbing her back. "Does he know?"

"Of course he knows," Avery said. "He would have been the first person she told."

"Yes," Aria confirmed. "I'd never keep him in the dark."

"Are you together?" Avery asked.

Aria was glad her friend's scowl was fixed on the wine rather than her. "No."

"Why not?" Now Avery shifted her steady gaze to Aria, who squirmed in her seat.

"It wasn't like that between us," she said. "We didn't have a relationship. We had a fling. Something I shouldn't have let happen in the first place."

"But you want more."

Aria shook her head, then nodded and shrugged. "Yes, no, maybe, I don't know. I would if he were anyone else. But he's an important guy. Rich. Powerful. You know how I feel about guys like that. Anyway, he's not interested. He thinks he would be a bad dad, and I know I'm all wrong for him."

"He'd be lucky to have you," Avery said matter-of-factly. "It's obvious he wants you, and you shouldn't deny yourself because of this bullshit phobia you have of powerful men."

Aria swallowed her surprise. "It's not bullshit. I have my reasons for feeling the way I do." Perfectly logical reasons based on past experience, not some random fear with no basis in the real world. "Anyway, he's not interested in me for anything more than sex."

Sophie rolled her eyes. "Are you nuts, Ri? He was sniffing after you as soon as he arrived. Of course he wants more than sex. You're lovely. How many times has he asked you out?"

"A couple," Aria admitted. "And thank you. But you're my friend. You have to say that. He doesn't want anything to do with me anymore. He wants to write a cheque once a month and send me on my way."

"Hey, cheer up." Sophie sat next to her and put an arm around her waist. "If anyone can convince him otherwise, it's you."

"Haven't you been listening? I don't want to change his mind." Her protest sounded weak.

"Of course you do," Avery said. "And you've got several months to do it."

Aria laughed. "You guys are insane. You know that, right? Okay, if I agree to consider it, will you stop talking? We've got a nursery to decorate."

"Seriously?" Sophie asked, grinning widely.

"Well, yeah. Why did you think I invited you here? I'm going to put you to work. I emptied out the spare room this morning and shifted everything into the garage. We've got a blank canvas, girls."

Even Avery cracked a smile. Before much longer they were busy, and by the end of the day, all that was missing from the nursery was a baby.

Aria sat back after her friends had left and smiled to herself. She was going to make this work, and she was going to be a kickass mother.

∿

IN THE DAYS since Aria had delivered the news, Eli had revised his budget, freeing up money to cover the exorbitant cost of a new baby, and rescheduled his time, allowing himself one weekend every two months to visit Itirangi. But he found himself wondering if he wanted to do more. Take a chance on being a father and a lover. With Aria around, he'd begun to feel like he could.

Eli missed her. He missed holding her close, missed her flamboyancy and spirit. She'd been a little ray of happiness and had lightened his heart. Bright, colorful and cheerful, she'd pulled him out of a slump and made him *want* something: *her*. He wanted her more than anything. He couldn't help it. He knew he didn't deserve her, and that his being with her would ruin their child's life, but Eli had never been good at letting go of something he wanted.

The phone rang, and his heart leapt. He snatched it off the bedside table, hoping to hear Aria's soft voice on the other end, but he was disappointed.

"Elijah, it's Frances here."

"Mother, why are you ringing at"—he checked his watch — "seven in the morning?"

"Did I wake you?"

"No," he sighed.

"Good. Any respectable businessman would have started his day by now."

Eli fought the urge to say something rude. He found he cared less and less for what respectable businessmen did. It was the weekend, for god's sake. "I'm sure they would, Mother."

"Frankly, I'm appalled at you," Frances said. "The house where you're staying is in a state of disrepair, and you allowed Therese to keep an animal and run wild with the *local* boys."

Eli wasn't brave enough to tell her he'd decided to keep the kitten. Well, actually, now a full-grown cat. The damn thing reminded him of Aria, and he enjoyed stroking it while sitting alone in his office late at night.

"Therese's teacher rang yesterday. It seems she's been more difficult than usual. When I spoke to her, she demanded to go back to Itirangi and attend public school. I had hoped you would be a good influence on her, but I do wonder if it didn't work out the other way around."

The flood of criticisms reminded Eli of his childhood. Nothing he'd done had ever been good enough. Damn, listening to her exhausted him.

"I won't be in Itirangi much longer," he replied. "But as far

143

as I'm concerned, Therese is welcome here for as long as I am. And honestly, Frances, what I do with myself really isn't your concern."

"As your mother, everything you do is my concern."

Eli held on to his patience. "What did you ring for, exactly?"

"You've been absent from the social scene for too long. There's a charity ball for the Breast Cancer Society next Saturday evening, eight o'clock, at the Herne Bay Yacht Club. Pick up Therese from school and bring her along. We need to restore your personal image, as well as my faith in you."

What a tempting offer. Eli hated public events. He hated being in the public eye, under pressure to do and say all the right things. Hated the endless stream of prospective wives Frances threw in his direction. The worst of these was Victoria Burns, who'd tired of her stint on the wild side, left the biker she'd cheated on him with, and befriended his mother to work her way back into his life. Victoria was a flawless blonde with a mercenary personality. Although he approved of mercenary tendencies in business partners, and even casual sex partners, Eli preferred his girlfriends to be softer. *More like Aria.*

The prospect of his mother thrusting another wife candidate under his nose made him shudder. He needed a shield, something to distract Frances. "Is there room at the table to bring a date?" he asked.

"Of course," Frances exclaimed. "I can arrange someone, if you'd like."

Eli cringed. "No need. I have someone in mind."

If Aria was going to have his child, she should formally meet the family. It would have to happen at some point, though he dreaded it. The thought of subjecting her to his judgmental parents horrified him. Their reaction to his change of circumstances would be extreme. And not in a good way.

"Oh?" Frances expressed her disbelief. "Are you dating someone?"

"Yes." God forgive him for the lie. It was necessary to preserve his sanity. "I'll bring her up with Therese. Does it suit for us to arrive at your place at five on Friday?"

"Yes, but—"

"I'm assuming it's a black-tie occasion?"

"Well, yes, but—"

"I'll see you then." Eli hung up, feeling quite pleased with himself.

CHAPTER 19

*A*ria added a sentence to her article about a new camping bylaw and glanced up as a messenger delivered a bouquet of red roses and darted off. He was gone before she could ask any questions. A card was tied around the stem of the bouquet, and she took it between her fingers to read the note. *I miss you.* She shut the roses in the kitchenette and pretended they didn't exist. Eli hadn't made any effort to see her since she'd broken the news, and she'd assumed his silence meant he had nothing more to say.

In the afternoon, a box of expensive chocolates arrived. She couldn't resist the urge to eat a few before hiding them away. Being sensitive to smell, it was increasingly difficult for her to enjoy food, so the sweets were a perfect pick-me-up.

Consumed by thoughts of Eli, she found it impossible to focus on her work. He was scheming something. But what? Was he trying to induce her to sleep with him again? Like 'Hey, you're pregnant already, so we may as well enjoy some more no-strings sex'. If so, then, no, thank you. They were linked together for life now, and no way was she making things more awkward by jumping right back into his bed.

That didn't mean she would *never* return to his bed. The idea of having a relationship with him had taken hold. Yes, he was a powerful man, but surely having his baby meant she was safe from him, that he'd go out of his way to protect her from rumors and humiliation. In which case, her reason for avoiding a relationship with him was moot. But she needed to play the long game. If she wanted Eli in her life, she needed to lure him back. She couldn't go to bed with him straight away, or he might lose interest.

Aria's patience was waning when, as she was packing up at the end of the day, the third package arrived. These gifts were just so damn confusing.

"What is it?" she snapped when the delivery boy hovered over her. He froze with a possum-in-the-headlights expression.

"Package for you, ma'am," he stammered.

"I'm sorry." It wasn't the boy's fault she was in a bad mood.

"That's all right, ma'am." He held out the package and rushed away as soon as she'd taken it.

Aria counted to ten before she unwrapped the parcel. It was small, decorated in pink paper with a white ribbon. The paper shredded easily, revealing a velvet box. Inside nestled a perfect ruby with a fine silver chain pooled around it. Aria gasped. The necklace was absolutely gorgeous. She ran a finger over its cool surface. It was deep and bloody, a shade of red she was partial to. The chain felt like silk between her fingers. She'd always preferred silver to gold, although she didn't know how Eli knew that. A lucky guess, perhaps.

But...what was she supposed to do with the necklace? She couldn't keep it. She snatched up the phone and called him.

"Good evening," he answered pleasantly.

"No," Aria snapped. "It's not. What do you think you're doing, sending me all these gifts? I'm returning the necklace to you tomorrow. I can't accept such an expensive present. Maybe you can get a refund."

Eli chuckled, sounding far too amused for her liking. "I'm not interested in a refund." His husky voice sent tingles up her spine.

"It's too much, Eli."

He ignored her. "I'd like you to wear the necklace to a charity ball my parents have invited me to on Saturday."

"Is that your way of asking me on a date?"

"You should meet my parents properly," he replied. "After all, you're giving them their first grandchild. Mother invited me, and it seemed like too good of an opportunity to miss. When I saw that necklace, I knew it would look perfect wrapped around your throat."

His words flustered her, but she kept a neutral tone. "I see your point about getting to know your parents better, but it's not necessary to buy me gifts. You're not trying to woo me. If you want me to spend time with your parents, just ask."

"Therese would love to have you there," he continued, unfazed. "She hasn't been to any society events before, and she's having problems at school. It would mean a lot to her if you came."

Aria sighed. "Are you trying to emotionally blackmail me? Using Teri to get your way?"

"The end justifies the means."

"What end did you have in mind?" she asked. "Are your parents supposed to love me, or hate me? I expect they won't be thrilled by the news. Have you told them?"

"No, I haven't. They'll be surprised, but it doesn't have to be a bad thing. The ball will be quick and painless. We can break the news, give them a chance to meet you, then get you home again. You will come, won't you?"

"Of course I'll come," she murmured. "I have a soft spot for you. Since we're stuck with each other long-term, I'd like to see how we suit. I know you don't agree, but I think you'll be a good dad."

"We have a lot of chemistry," Eli replied. "But having a baby complicates things. I know my own shortcomings, and I won't make my child live with a bad parent." Regret was evident in his tone of voice. Misguided as he was, his decision hadn't come easily.

Aria couldn't listen to him any longer. It was too much. "I don't want to argue with you. Let me know when we're leaving for Auckland." She disconnected the call and tried to disconnect her heart. Alas, it seemed determined to desire the unobtainable.

~

LATE SATURDAY MORNING, Eli pulled up outside Aria's house as she waited on the couch on the porch. She'd spent hours thinking about the upcoming trip. Eli obviously didn't think they were compatible, but she didn't share his view. Going home with him that day on the beach had been a bad idea, but the cat was out of the bag now, and although they were very different people, if they worked hard, they could make something of their relationship. If only he was willing. On this trip, Aria hoped to convince him to give them a chance.

On top of worrying endlessly about breaking the news to his parents, she'd also spent a lot of time debating what to wear. Everything she knew about Frances and Phillip indicated that the event they were attending would be formal and glamorous. The nicest item in her closest was a lilac chiffon dress she'd worn when she was a bridesmaid, and she had the feeling that, pretty though it was, it wouldn't be up to scratch. She'd made a phone call to her friend Clarissa, a bridal designer, and explained the situation, knowing she could trust Rissa to save her. Luckily, her friend had just the dress for the occasion.

"Aria."

The rich voice sent a shiver racing down her spine, but she smiled casually in response, determined to play it cool. "Eli."

He looked immaculate this morning, wearing a tailored suit that was no doubt meant to impress his parents. If his success so far hadn't impressed them, she doubted anything could, but she approved of the suit anyway. The way it embraced his broad shoulders made her weak at the knees.

"Are you all packed?" he asked.

Aria nodded. "Ready to go."

Sliding into the front seat of Eli's Mercedes, she slipped on her sunglasses. "What will it be like tonight?"

"Nothing exciting," he replied. "We'll arrive, listen to some speeches, eat dinner and listen to some more speeches. There will be dancing and socializing until the end of the night. My mother likes to stay until things wind down, which is about two in the morning."

THEY DROVE to the airport in silence. Aria grew more anxious the closer they came to boarding the plane. She hated flying. Abhorred it. Being hundreds of feet in the air in a tiny tube, while her stomach churned, was not her idea of a good time. Pretty much the opposite.

After they took their seats (first class, of course), she chewed furiously on gum, a habit that seemed to help. The plane began to move, and Aria closed her eyes, reminding herself it was only a short flight. An hour and a half, tops. But when the plane shook as it left the ground, she couldn't keep calm anymore and grabbed Eli's hand—big, sturdy and oddly reassuring. He gaped at her, and although she was mortified, she couldn't let go.

"You're afraid of flying?" he asked, his breath tickling her ear as he leaned closer.

"Yes." She thought he'd laugh at her or make a joke, but, instead, he looked at their intertwined hands, at her white knuckles, and squeezed. Encouraged by his quiet support, she tried to explain. "I get really sick. I always take pills, but sometimes they don't work. I prefer to keep my feet on the ground."

Eli nodded and gently stroked her hand with his thumb. "Why didn't you tell me?"

She watched his thumb skim over her hand. "It's embarrassing. Pathetic. What sort of grown woman is scared of flying?"

He grasped her chin with his other hand and lifted it to look into her eyes. "One of the best women I know."

Her heart skipped a beat, and her stomach filled with butterflies dancing a samba. The way he was looking at her was so...well, she didn't quite know what. The light in his eyes could have been admiration, or even adoration. But surely not. She was certain he desired her, but anything else was a different matter entirely.

"I care about you," he continued, speaking quietly so as not to draw any attention, and it felt startlingly intimate. "You're going to be the mother of my child. Most women would have panicked when they discovered they were pregnant, but you've been level-headed and brave. So what if you have a little fear of flying? You can hold my hand for as long as you like."

Despite her gut telling her it was a very bad idea, Aria did hold his hand all the way to Auckland.

CHAPTER 20

*E*li couldn't believe it. The woman who had put him in his place more than once, and had fearlessly told him she was carrying his baby, was shaking in her seat. It boggled his mind, but the panic he saw was real, and it pleased him to be able to distract her for a time. With her big personality, it was easy to forget she wasn't ten feet tall and invincible. Feeling her small hand inside his had kicked his protective instincts into gear, and he'd wanted to take her in his arms and make her forget her fear.

She was vulnerable; he liked that. The women he usually dated wouldn't allow anyone to see their weaknesses. Instead, they hid them behind masks of cool civility.

When they got off the plane, Aria looked up at him with gratitude, and he felt positively heroic, the urge to flex his muscles and claim her as his own almost overwhelming. He wanted her. He'd wanted her from the moment he'd first seen her, but at that moment, he *really* wanted her. His fingernails bit into his palms as he stopped himself from reaching out to her; gathering her into his arms would be a mistake of epic proportions. She was soon to be a mother, which meant she was off-limits to him. When he finally settled down, he needed a woman who would be content without children—then his expected failure as a parent could never be tested. But still, Aria's eyes, shining with emotion, and the knowledge of his baby growing inside of her sent a surge of possessiveness sweeping through him. Eli had never been a jealous lover, but he resolved that if any other man laid a hand on Aria, he would destroy them.

~

TERI RACED over to Aria when she and Eli entered the foyer of the apartment building and threw her arms around her. "I've missed you so much!"

Aria stepped backwards with the force of the impact. "Whoa. I've missed you too, sweetie."

Teri leaned closer and muttered, "I've been stuck at school for weeks. It's hell."

Aria laughed. "You're out now. We get to dress up and go to a ball together. It'll be like a fairy tale."

"I'm just happy to get out of there," Teri said.

Aria stifled a laugh. "It can't be that bad. Now, don't be so gloomy. We're going to have a good time."

"Maybe," Teri mumbled. "But only because you're here."

"Thank you." Aria was touched, and she knew that even if the meeting with Mr. and Mrs. Lockwood went pear-shaped, Teri would be on her side. The girl would be a great aunt.

AS THEY ENTERED Eli's apartment, sunlight warmed his skin, beaming into the living room through the glass walls. He deposited his bag in the bedroom, which boasted a perfectly made bed with hospital corners and the coverlet folded back. When he returned to the lounge, Teri was heading for the exit.

"I'm going to see Kelly," she said on her way out, referring to her friend who lived down the hall.

"Be back before three," he called. "You need to be here to get ready for tonight."

With a quick nod, she was out the door. Eli led Aria, who'd returned from the guest bedroom, into the lounge.

Her eyes were bright and her cheeks flushed. "This place is fantastic. I can't believe you have a personal spa bath. I'm so jealous."

"Are you?" he asked, his imagination firing up with pictures of the erotic things he could do with her in a spa.

"It looks wonderful. Can I use it later?"

He smiled. "Absolutely. I'm glad you like it." He wondered if he could convince her to move into this apartment permanently. It had occurred to him that having Aria in Auckland would be much more convenient than being separated by half the length of the country.

She walked over to the wall where he knew the view over the harbor was superb. "I love it," she said. "And the view is gorgeous."

The light played across her curls, and when she turned to smile at him, the air whooshed from his lungs. She was the most beautiful thing he'd ever seen. Eli crossed the room and slid an arm around her waist, facing the water with her. Dozens of white yachts were floating on the water, and Waiheke Island was green on the horizon.

Aria tucked an errant curl behind her ear, brushing him as she moved. Her touch made his gut clench with desire. His arm tightened around her waist, and before he could overthink the action, he drew her closer to him and lowered his lips to hers. He tasted her slowly and sweetly, glorying in the way she wound her arms around his neck, pressing herself against him. Her hands burrowed beneath his shirt and smoothed over his stomach, and his muscles quivered as she explored him with her fingers. She tugged on his shirt, and he met her eyes, watching desire flare in them.

"I'm sorry," he murmured. "You looked like an angel."

She stroked her hand over the outside of his trousers.

He shook his head. "We should stop."

"I know," she said. "But I've missed you."

When she said things like that, she challenged his sanity. As if they had a mind of their own, his fingers fumbled with his shirt buttons, and when his shirt hung open, Aria pushed it from his shoulders and ran her hands greedily over him. Eli closed his eyes and fought his growing need. He couldn't be with her. Look what had happened the last time they'd been careless.

Stop, you idiot.

She wasn't making it easy for him to resist, though. With her small fingers feathering over his body, he was tempted to grab her and show her she was playing with fire.

All of a sudden, the hands left him. He felt bereft.

"No, you're right," she said. Her chest rose and fell rapidly, and her nipples protruded through the fabric of her top. "We need to stop."

The words made no sense. All Eli could see were those heaving breasts, the lips that were puffy from his kisses, and the eyes that just begged for more.

"Aw, hell," he muttered, returning to her mouth, then pulling away. "What if we just do it once?"

"Only once?" she echoed, pressed against the length of his body. "You promise?"

"Cross my heart."

"Okay."

~

SHE KNEW she should behave more responsibly, but Eli was so damned appealing, with his kind words and hot body.

155

Frankly, she didn't want to be responsible, and part of her couldn't resist the thought of being reckless with him again. *Go after what you want, girl.*

When he'd appeared at her cottage, looking untouchable, she'd wanted to run her hands through his hair, ruffle his clothes and muss him up. Now, she melted against his naked chest, loving the roughness of the hair beneath her fingers. Craving skin-on-skin contact, she pulled her top off and pressed her stomach against his. She slid her hand beneath his waistband and took him in her hand, delighted when a shudder ran through him as she tightened her grip and stroked.

"Aria," he groaned, his forehead resting on hers, his breathing uneven. "Sweetheart."

Feeling powerful, she continued stroking up and down his shaft. His breath came in shallow gasps, and she kissed him softly. His eyes opened, blazing into hers. When he gathered her up against him and lifted her, she wrapped her legs around his waist. He backed her up against the wall. Gripping his hair, she met him kiss for kiss. His pelvis ground against her in the right way, and she wanted more of it. So much more.

"The bed," she urged.

"No," he said. "Here."

He lowered her to her feet and dropped to his knees, pulling her leggings down bit by bit, kissing and nipping her skin as it became exposed. He lifted her shirt, pushed the fabric back and pressed his cheek against her soft belly.

"Mine," he whispered.

"Yes," she said, closing her eyes and leaning against the wall for support. Eli nuzzled her stomach, and she whimpered. "Now," she said. "Please, Eli."

"No," he said gruffly. "It's my turn to tease you."

He moved lower, still licking and nuzzling, and a peak of

pleasure built within her. She didn't know how much more of this she could take.

"Please," she begged.

"You are so sexy," he groaned as he slipped his pants down, lifted her to his waist, and sheathed himself inside her.

Slowly, he began to move, going deeper and deeper until she thought he'd become part of her. Then his thrusts became frenzied, and Aria cried out as the world fractured into a million blissful pieces. A moment later, he stiffened and dropped his head to her shoulder, panting in her ear.

"That was amazing," Aria murmured.

"We shouldn't have done it."

Not exactly what she wanted to hear while she was sated in his arms. The words were indisputable, though. She ought not to have been with Eli *again*. It was too late to take it back, so she wriggled to the floor and led him to the bed. He wrapped his arms around her and tugged her against him.

Aria loved being spooned, feeling another person's heart-beat and sharing their warmth. Eli Lockwood was a really good big spoon. Strong and safe. It was silly, but she couldn't help feeling that way. Sometime later, lost in her thoughts, she drifted off to sleep.

THIS TIME, it was Aria who woke to a cold bed. Eli was gone, and a scrap of paper lay on his pillow. She leaned over to read the note.

You look beautiful when you sleep. Being together was a mistake, but I don't regret it. I set the alarm to wake you up in time for the hairdresser at 3pm.

Eli

Checking the time, she realized she had ten minutes to get dressed and tidy up before the hairdresser arrived. A smile touched her lips. That man thought of everything. What would it be like to relax and let him take care of her for a few days? It was too tempting. As she lay tangled in the sheets, grinning over memories of the things they'd done, she realized she was in danger of losing her heart.

The smiled faded from her lips. She couldn't let herself get attached to him. Eli would move on without a second thought, except for a slight pinch in the pocket from his monthly child support payments, and she wasn't the type to recover easily from being left behind.

DURING TWO HOURS OF PAMPERING, every one of her hairs was either put in place or removed, and she was scrubbed and smothered with a hundred different lotions and pastes. The dress stayed in the wardrobe while she was prepared, and then she transferred it back to her suitcase when they were ready to leave. She understood they were visiting Eli's parents' house before carrying on to the ball, so she didn't want to put her dress on too early and risk spilling something on it.

She met Eli and Teri at the door. Teri, wearing a layer of pale makeup with silver eyeshadow and pink lip gloss, wasn't dressed yet either. Eli looked much the same as earlier. When their gazes locked, his eyes darkened, and heat pooled in her stomach.

"We can stop somewhere on the way and buy you a dress," he said.

"I have one," she replied.

"I'm sure you do," he said agreeably, but doubt clouded his features.

"I have a dress that's perfect for the occasion," she insisted. "I don't need you to buy me one."

"Are you sure?"

"Yes." End of matter. Case closed.

He didn't argue, for which she was thankful. However,

she couldn't help but be offended by his lack of belief that she was capable of clothing herself correctly.

"All right." His lips twitched into a smile, which made her want to kiss the corner of his mouth. "Let's go, then."

THE TRIP TO HIS PARENTS' house took only twenty minutes. Aria, prepared to be impressed by his childhood home, was stunned instead. The driveway, edged by cherry trees, continued for nearly a kilometer. They drove past a well-tended garden which covered at least two acres of land, a tennis court, and an outdoor pool. The house, when they finally reached the end of the driveway, was enormous: at least three stories tall, with expanses of glass, metal, and monochromatic tiles. Eli parked next to a fountain featuring a naked water nymph and helped her out of the car.

They walked to the door with her hand tucked inside his elbow, and Teri trailed behind, seeming reluctant to be back home. With each step, Aria sensed Eli growing tenser.

"Get ready to meet my parents," he said.

"I've already met them," Aria responded, confused.

"On their home turf, as my date and with...everything else, it's a totally different story."

"Oh." She'd been nervous before, but now it was like a sliver of ice had passed through her lungs, and she couldn't draw breath. "How angry will they be?"

He stopped, pressed a kiss to her forehead and said, "It will be fine."

Teri gagged. "Get a room!"

Nausea curled in her gut as she walked toward the stylish home where Eli had grown up. She felt sick and so, so scared. Her stomach fluttered, and she rubbed it absent-mindedly.

We'll be okay, baby. Your mummy is strong. For her baby, she would fight dragons. What were a couple of entrepreneurs compared to that?

CHAPTER 21

A compact woman with a sour expression met them at the door and escorted them to a small lounge where Frances and Phillip were waiting.

"Mother. Father," Eli greeted them politely.

Aria compared their formality to the familiarity of her own family, where hugs were frequent, personal space was non-existent, and the words 'I love you' were bandied about. Never one to stand on ceremony, she knew which situation she preferred.

Teri remained silent, subdued, as she had been since they got into the car. Aria had chalked it up to nerves over the upcoming ball, but now, she wondered if it had more to do with the strained relationship between the Lockwood siblings and their parents.

"Hi, Mr. and Mrs. Lockwood," she said with a forced smile. "It's nice to see you again."

"You," Phillip Lockwood said, raising a finger to point at her. "I know you. Where have I seen you before?"

"Aria cooked for you when you visited me in Itirangi," Eli explained, wrapping an arm around her shoulders so she couldn't move from his side.

"You're his cook?" Frances asked, already scowling in disapproval.

"No," Aria corrected, wondering why it would be so bad if she were. "I was doing him a favor that night. I'm a journalist."

"Are you working on something for my son?" Frances asked. "Why are you here?"

"Aria is my date," Eli said, raising his chin as if daring them to comment. She noticed he didn't say she was pregnant and wondered when he planned to break the news.

"How long have you been seeing each other?"

The expression in his mother's eyes suggested she was an unwelcome complication.

"Since I've been in Itirangi," Eli replied. He was stretching the truth, but if he wanted to lie to his parents, that was his business.

"How fortunate for you to receive such a lovely welcome." Frances' words were clipped. Clearly, she believed Aria was a gold-digger. But what else could she think when she believed they'd been together from the first moment he'd arrived in town? When she found out about the pregnancy, it would only confirm her suspicions. Aria didn't blame her, but it hurt. What did annoy her was the implication that women were attracted to Eli for his money. Had Frances taken a good look at her son recently? Or spoken to him? He was sexy and sweet, practically catnip to most women.

"Yes," Eli replied. Aria begun to suspect he was intentionally baiting his mother. "As soon as I met her, I knew she was special, and I haven't let go since."

Aria didn't like the direction the conversation was taking, or the lies he was telling, so she interrupted. "You have a lovely home, Mrs. Lockwood. Your gardens are gorgeous. It must be wonderful during the summer."

No one replied. A girl wearing an apron and white gloves entered with a tray of herbal tea and the most delightful miniature scones Aria had ever seen. She helped herself to one and found it tasted as good as it looked. Then she noticed everybody's eyes had widened in shock and Frances' jaw had gone slack. Apparently, this wasn't a 'help yourself' kind of place. As if to diffuse the tension, Teri also grabbed a scone and bit into it.

Eli moved to a couch, taking Aria with him. The server poured tea, and they sipped while Eli made awkward small talk with his parents. They discussed his new project, the family business, and a holiday that Frances and Phillip would soon be taking to Bora Bora.

Aria felt like a stranger in a strange land. She didn't understand this family, and she wasn't sure how to behave. It was like they all had a copy of some etiquette manual, but no one had shared it with her.

When it was time to change for the ball, Eli showed her to a spare bedroom where she could get herself ready. Teri stayed with her.

"That was awful," Teri exclaimed when they were in private.

"It wasn't so bad," Aria said, although secretly she felt shaken.

"It actually was," Teri argued. "They're like robots. *Snobby* robots. I hate being back here."

"They're a bit uptight," Aria admitted. "But you shouldn't say disrespectful things about them. They are your parents, after all." She unzipped her bag and added, "Come on, let's see your dress."

Teri opened her bag and pulled out a pale pink gown. She changed into it quickly and twirled. The gown fell to her ankles and was strapless with a fitted bodice and diamantes adorning the skirt. Paired with a seven-lucky-rings necklace and silver wedge heels, she looked radiant.

"You're stunning," Aria gushed.

Teri was gorgeous in a classic way, with her light hair

hanging around her shoulders in loose curls, a heart-shaped face and deep blue eyes. She tried to hide herself behind makeup and a feisty attitude, but that only went so far.

"Let's see yours," Teri said, uncomfortable with the attention, but also smiling a secretly pleased smile.

Aria stripped off and wriggled into the dress Clarissa had sent her. It was as long as Teri's dress and made from midnight blue silk with a neckline that plunged, but not indecently so. Simple and elegant. She had loved it on sight.

Apparently, Teri did too, because she clapped her hands together gleefully and said, "Eli's going to *die* when he sees you in that."

ELI WAS STANDING RIGIDLY next to the front door when Therese and Aria emerged from the spare room. After a cursory glance at his sister, he turned to his lover, and his breath squeezed out of his chest as he absorbed the sight of her. The dress hugged her curves and swayed with her hips as she walked. Her cleavage teased him from the narrowly plunging neckline. Her lips were pursed, painted a fierce red, and her hair, which he'd barely noticed earlier, was tamed into an elegant twist that cascaded down the side of her neck. She stole his breath. The outfit was missing something, though. Before he realized he was doing it, he'd crossed to her side and taken her hand in his.

"You look beautiful," he said. "Absolutely beautiful."

He pulled a box from his pocket and handed it to her, watching anxiously as she opened it to reveal a blue topaz necklace on a silver chain.

"What's this?" she asked, turning her shining eyes up to his.

"I wanted you to have something to wear with your

163

dress," he said. "Since you refused to bring the other necklace, I thought you might like this one. It suits you."

She picked up the chain and ran her fingers over it.

"Do you like it?" he asked.

"Yes," she said softly. "Thank you."

He let out a deep breath. He hadn't realized how much it would mean to hear she liked it. Finally, he'd done something right.

"Here." He took the necklace from her and draped it around her neck, fumbling with the clasp because her nearness flustered him.

"So sweet," Teri mocked, screwing up her nose.

Eli stepped back and cleared his throat. "Shall we get going?"

ARIA CHATTED to Teri during the long drive across town to the yacht club, imagining what the ball would be like. She hadn't been to one since high school, and that had been pretty relaxed. Tonight, she expected something completely different.

Dozens of lanterns illuminated the entrance to the venue, and white sails flew overhead, light and ethereal. They walked up a short flight of stairs to the massive door, which was at least fifteen feet tall. Already, Aria was awed. A small gaggle of reporters was hovering outside, trapping each group before they moved through the threshold.

A tall, slender couple were speaking to the cameras thirty yards in front of them, and Aria wondered if they were famous. She never thought she'd be sharing a room with celebrities. How thrilling. As they strolled toward the door, she did her best to glide smoothly in her stiletto heels, but she'd never been graceful, so she scuffed her toes more than once.

A reporter and a cameraman broke away from the group and approached them.

"Mr. Lockwood," the reporter called. "We spoke to your parents earlier. Can you confirm you're here with them tonight?"

"Yes," Eli replied as the reporter thrust the microphone in his face. "I'm attending with my parents."

His calm demeanor impressed Aria. He came across as utterly urbane and aristocratic, holding his shoulders back with his hair brushed away from his face, highlighting his strong cheekbones and deep blue eyes. Untouchable. Except he wasn't. She shivered, remembering the way those eyes had flared with heat when he'd kissed her. She'd seen him out of control, and she liked it.

"This is the first event you've attended with your parents in several months," the reporter remarked. "Why is that?"

"I've been living on a different island, so naturally, I haven't seen much of my parents recently." He nodded to the reporter with finality, ending the brief interview, and continued toward the entrance. His palm, a gentle heat in the small of Aria's back, urged her on.

When she passed through the door and gazed out over the ballroom, she gasped. They'd stepped onto a wooden dance floor flanked by tables of finger foods. A dozen feet up, a platform surrounded the edge of the room. At the far end of the room, between the dance floor and the platform, a stage was set. No fewer than two hundred people were milling about, a few seated at tables on the upper level and the rest standing on the ballroom floor. Even at first glance, Aria could tell these men and women were wealthy. She felt gauche and unrefined by comparison.

"Wow," she breathed. "This is totally intimidating."

"You'll be fine," Eli said, rubbing comforting circles on her back. "Don't worry."

Teri grabbed her arm, eyes glittering with excitement. "This is so cool."

"Don't get too excited," Aria teased. "Someone might think you're enjoying yourself." She turned to Eli. "Should we find your parents?"

"Not yet," he replied. "Let's enjoy ourselves while we can." He glanced at his watch. "Dinner begins at eight. Until then, we're free to look around."

"Everything sparkles," Teri murmured, leaning toward Aria, who squeezed her hand.

"So do we," Aria said. "You look gorgeous. I bet every young guy in here is looking at you."

"They'd better not be," Eli grumbled, steering them farther into the room.

Aria found she liked being at his side. Not a single one of the well-dressed men could rival Eli, and he drew admiring gazes from most of the women. While she liked being next to the sexiest man in the room, she was also uncomfortable receiving so much attention—glares from women and assessing glances from men. Thank god this wasn't part of her day-to-day life. Having so many women lusting after her man would be a nightmare. Not that Eli was *her* man. But she could pretend, for one night—like Cinderella with her prince, except instead of an evil stepmother, there was an evil mother-in-law. She grinned at the thought.

ELI STRODE THROUGH THE CROWD, sweeping Aria along beside him, with Therese shuffling behind. He'd spotted Victoria Burns across the room conversing with his parents and knew instantly that his mother had set this up, hoping to divide him from Aria. *And she doesn't even know about the pregnancy yet.*

He had no interest in reuniting with his old flame. Not

when he was burning for Aria alone. And for god's sake, Victoria had humiliated him in front of every reader of *The Star* magazine, and every person those readers gossiped to. How could Frances even contemplate a reunion between them?

A voice over the loudspeaker announced it was time to take their seats, so he led Therese and Aria to their table; as a man who liked to be prepared, he'd located it earlier in the night. They hadn't yet sat when Frances and Phillip headed toward them with a third person in tow. He groaned out loud.

"Are you okay?" Aria asked, concerned. The poor woman didn't realize just how awkward the night was about to become.

"The woman with my parents is my ex-girlfriend," he muttered. Shame welled up inside him that his parents would play such a dirty trick. Though he could handle it, Aria shouldn't have to.

"Your ex-girlfriend?" she asked, her voice strained.

"Yes," he confirmed, pressing her closer to his side.

"She's gorgeous."

He hated how disturbed she sounded. Yes, Victoria was attractive, but she didn't have nearly as much heart as Aria. He didn't desire her with the same intensity, and never had.

"You're more gorgeous," he replied, and then ground his teeth together in frustration when she raised a dubious eyebrow.

"She's a hell-bitch," Therese said matter-of-factly.

"Teri!" Aria scolded, but Eli thought she sounded pleased. Odd; he'd never realized his little sister had such strong feelings about Victoria.

Eli, Therese and Aria took their seats at the table. Five seats remained—three for his parents and Victoria. His parents' lawyer Dave and his wife Christine claimed the remaining two.

"Elijah, Therese," his mother greeted them as they got settled. "You remember Dave and Christine?" She directed the question to Eli, who nodded. "And of course you know Victoria."

He tilted his head to acknowledge the statuesque blonde. "Good evening, Victoria."

"Oh, come now, Elijah." She spoke in dulcet tones, reaching out to take his hand, the movement jangling the bracelets on her wrist and pulling the sleek black dress she was wearing tighter across her midriff. She had always been elegant, and tonight she'd pulled out all the stops. What sort of ideas had his mother planted in her head? "No need to be so formal. We have history, after all. Why don't you introduce me to your delightful friend?"

He'd rather chew on nails, but it didn't seem as if he had much choice.

"This is Aria Simons," he said reluctantly. "Aria, this is Victoria Burns."

"Daughter of William Burns, the founder of Burns Technologies," Frances added. "Victoria is their Director of Marketing."

"Nice to meet you," Aria said politely, but her hand gripped Eli's knee under the table, and he thought he saw a shadow pass across her face.

"Delighted," Victoria replied, her expression indicating that she was anything but. Her eyes narrowed further when Eli took Aria's hand from his knee and laid it on the table, his fingers intertwined with hers. "I hear you live in the little town where Elijah is working at the moment."

A waiter appeared at her elbow and began filling drinks.

"Yes," Aria replied. "I grew up in Itirangi and moved back about a year ago."

Eli wondered what had prompted her to move back. She had the skills and the drive to do better than write community interest articles in a provincial newspaper. Was it related

168

to the rumors that she'd slept with her boss? He didn't believe it of her, no matter what Mark Talbot's opinion might be, but the thought of her with anyone else—let alone a man who might have taken advantage of her—made his chest ache. He rubbed it absently with his free hand.

"I don't imagine there's much in Itirangi except for sheep and grass," Victoria remarked snidely.

"And cows," Aria replied, seemingly unbothered by the comment. "We have a lot of cows. Don't forget about them."

Eli snorted into his wine, earning reproachful looks from both his mother and Victoria, but Aria smiled, and his heart thumped erratically in response. His gut told him it would be all downhill from there.

CHAPTER 22

*A*fter the mention of cows, Victoria ignored Aria, as if she was beneath her notice. The Lockwood parents began discussing business, excluding Aria from the conversation—probably a deliberate ploy by Frances to make her son see that Aria was unsuitable.

"And then," Frances continued, "Kevin declared it the most thought-provoking campaign since the Waldorf affair in 2014."

Eli leaned toward Aria. "Kevin is the chief executive officer of—"

"Pish, Elijah, I'm sure Amelia isn't interested in our little business discussions," Frances interrupted, then turned back to the rest of the table. "Of course, I said to Kevin…"

Aria tuned out of the conversation. She couldn't understand why Frances disliked her so much—she didn't even know her—but her attitude was upsetting. Especially when she contemplated how a lifetime of their condescension would feel for her baby, who'd done nothing to deserve it.

A young waitress served the entrée, which appeared to be a bald sparrow. Aria choked on bile at the sight of it. There was no salad, nothing else she could eat. She stayed silent, dredged up a smile for the waitress and sipped her orange juice instead.

"Is there something wrong with your quail?" Victoria asked.

"No, but I'm vegetarian," Aria explained. "I'll wait for the main. I'm sure there will be something I can eat."

A hush fell over the table, and she wondered what unspoken rule of etiquette she'd broken now.

"Don't you like meat?" Dave asked, breaking the awkward silence.

"To be honest, I don't remember. It's been so long since I ate it." The pungent scent of it was certainly putting her off at the moment.

"Aria is a vegetarian because she thinks it's wrong to eat animals," Teri piped up for the first time during the evening. "She volunteers at the animal shelter back in Itirangi. She gave me the kitten to look after for a while."

A kitten that Aria had noticed Eli had kept. Obviously, he hadn't told Teri, though.

"So, it's you we have to thank for that lovely creature?" Frances queried, her grimace saying it made perfect sense.

Aria felt compelled to defend herself. "I think having a pet teaches people about being responsible and caring for others."

"It teaches people how to clean up someone else's mess," Frances said. "That isn't a lesson Therese needs."

"My dear," Phillip began, "I think you would like meat if you tried it now. It's understandable you would have a bad impression of it if your mother didn't cook well, or if cooking isn't your forte."

"I enjoy cooking," Aria said. "And I like to think I'm good at it. I certainly haven't had any complaints. If you'll excuse me, I need to find the ladies' room."

She got away from the table as quickly as possible, gaining some much-needed distance. People often questioned her diet. She lived in a farming town, so she was used to it. But having her diet, her hometown, and her cooking abilities all called into question within an hour was a new experience. Frankly, keeping a straight spine in the face of their animosity was exhausting her.

Once in the ladies' room, she studied herself in the mirror. Her face appeared pale behind a layer of foundation, washed out. She reapplied lipstick, dotted some color onto her checks, and twisted her lips into a smile.

"You can do this," she said. "You're a strong woman."

Great. Now she sounded like one of her mother's self-affirmation DVDs. She gave herself two thumbs up before heading back to the table. When she was a few feet away, she heard her name and hesitated. No one had noticed her, so she edged toward the wall, trying to blend in, and listened intently.

"Aria is a charming girl," Victoria was saying. "So provincial. It's sweet of you to bond with the locals, Elijah."

"That's not—"

"She cooks some hearty meals, does she? She certainly keeps herself full-figured."

Aria gasped. Then she looked down at herself. Sure, her hips were wide, her butt prominent and her boobs more than a handful, but she exercised regularly, and she was in good shape. For god's sake, she was pregnant. Shouldn't they cut her a bit of slack?

A flush crept up her neck. Victoria, slender as a stick, clearly thought all women were meant to be that way. At that moment, a waitress stepped too close and Aria tripped over her feet, drawing the attention of everyone seated at the table. Teri covered her mouth in horror, and Eli's expression was stony— perhaps he was angry; it was difficult to tell— but no one else seemed concerned. She was torn between pretending she didn't care and stomping away. Leaving would be far more satisfying, but it would also be childish, and she didn't have anywhere to go.

Instead of running, she took her seat, flashed a big smile at Victoria Burns, and said, "I *am* a great cook, and I *do* have a full figure. I rather like it. I'm not a size six, but so what? Different strokes for different folks." She enjoyed the astonishment that flickered across Victoria's face. Aria didn't like conflict, but she wasn't a doormat, and she wasn't about to be treated like one.

Victoria tilted her head and plastered on a phony smile. "So true."

Teri giggled, and her hands shook. Luckily, before further words could be spoken, the main meal arrived. Ham, with a side portion of potatoes and a green salad. Thank-freaking-god. Aria was starving.

They ate in silence and sat through speeches that went on for far too long. Dessert followed. Half of the dessert bowls held fruit salads, and the rest held towers of ice cream. Aria quickly snagged one of the bowls of ice cream and took a mouthful. Heavenly. A tangy lemon flavor incited her taste buds and slid smoothly down her throat.

She heard a snigger and glanced up. Everyone was watching her.

"What?" she demanded. Any patience she'd had left was rapidly drying up.

"Are you trying to eat it or have sex with it, darling?" Victoria sneered.

"Ask Eli. He'd know." Dave chuckled. He wasn't being malicious, but his thoughtless comment made Aria uncomfortable.

"For god's sake!" Eli exclaimed, laying down his cutlery with a clang. "Can't you be civil for a couple of hours?"

Aria kept her head down.

"Elijah, we want to know how long this phase is going to

last," his mother said as if it was the most reasonable thing in the world.

"What phase?" Eli asked. His nostrils flared, and he'd gone rigid, like a predator posed to pounce on its prey. His fingers twitched, and he shoved them beneath the table.

"Dating inappropriate women," Frances said. "Luckily for you, Victoria will still be here for you when you're over it, and she won't hold it against you. You should really appreciate that."

"I can't believe you said that in front of Aria," Eli growled. "I thought you would at least try to act like a decent human being. I guess I was hoping for too much. And *Victoria*?" His voice lowered to a hiss. "You think she's 'appropriate'?" He added air quotations. "How appropriate was she when she was screwing another man on the back of a motorcycle in an alley outside a nightclub?"

Victoria paled.

Frances tutted. "We all make mistakes."

Aria's head swung back and forward between them. She couldn't believe this was happening. Her family teased each other, but they rarely fought.

"I've had enough of this." Eli stood and grabbed her by the elbow. His fingers were rough, and she winced but allowed him to pull her up. "Let's go."

Teri awkwardly shuffled to her feet, interlocking her fingers with Aria's.

"Don't you think you're overreacting, Elijah?" Frances asked.

"No," he said stiffly. "I don't. Aria is pregnant, Mother. She's having my baby, and I intend to raise it with her. She *will* be in my life for the foreseeable future, so you had better accustom yourself to the idea."

"*What?*" Teri gasped, smacking her thigh with her palm.

"You've got this little country tramp pregnant?" Frances sounded ready to explode.

174

HIS MOTHER APPEARED to be hyperventilating. Too bad. He'd been patient with her when she'd demanded he look after Teri for the summer, and when she'd brought Victoria with her tonight, knowing he'd come with a date. In fact, he'd been patient with her for his whole damned life. But he'd reached the end of his tether when his mother insulted the woman he loved.

Hang on. He loved her? Yeah, maybe he did. At least, he was very fond of her.

"Aria is not a tramp," he fumed. The tremble of her arm made him want to hurt someone. "She's a sweet, successful woman, and she's going to be a wonderful mother."

Saying the words made him realize he wanted to be there to see it. The day-to-day raising of their child, the long nights, the first words... He wanted to share all of it with her. There would be no joint custody, no dysfunctional upbringing for his kid. The more he considered it, the more he liked the idea. Life would never be boring with Aria around. They could move into his apartment together, and he'd make sure that his child and his wife had the best care available. He liked the thought of taking care of her.

He smiled down at her. "You're amazing."

She returned the smile, hers tremulous. "Thank you."

How much had it cost her to stand next to him and bear these insults? A weaker woman would have run by now. Everything about her impressed him.

"You can't be serious!" Frances cried. "She's not even remotely suitable. She probably got pregnant on purpose to get her greedy little paws on your money."

"Don't speak about her like that," Eli warned, becoming aware of the scene they were causing; the occupants of the surrounding tables were watching curiously. "You may be my mother, but if you ask me to choose between you and my child, you're going to lose."

"How dare you!"

"Why don't we all calm down?" Phillip suggested. "Frances, breathe. Elijah, it's understandable that you feel obligated to the girl, but that doesn't mean you have to stay with her. These days, it's not a big deal for a woman to be a single mother. You can support her financially; I would expect nothing less. But you don't have to tie yourself to her for the rest of your life."

"With all possible respect, it's my choice," Eli replied tersely, disturbed by how closely the words echoed his earlier sentiments. "I'll do as I see fit. I came here to do you the courtesy of letting you know you're going to be grandparents."

He took a deep breath to calm his racing heart. He might be ruthless in his business dealings, but he'd never stood up to his parents the way he had tonight. Suddenly, while staring down the people who'd raised him, he realized he would never treat his son or daughter the way they had treated him. In fact, he wouldn't treat anyone the way they'd treated him. He had more decency than his parents.

He wasn't them.

He was his own person, with his own failings, and he was sure to fail in some respects when raising his child, but they wouldn't be the same ways his parents had failed with him. He would never let his child think they weren't good enough or leave them waiting for hours after school because he didn't have enough time to pick them up. Eli was different from his parents, and he wasn't going to let them ruin his relationship with his kid before it even started.

"I'll speak to you again in a few weeks," he told them. "Meanwhile, think about how highly you want to prioritize having a relationship with your grandchild."

*a*s they left the yacht club through the fifteen-foot door, Aria's pulse was racing a million miles an hour. She'd never been defended by anyone other than family before. It felt wonderful, but unsettling too. The cool night air prickled her arms, and goosebumps skittered over her skin. Eli shrugged out of his jacket and wrapped it around her shoulders.

"So..." Teri drew the word out. "That went well. Uh, when were you guys planning to tell me about the bundle of joy?"

"Later," Eli snapped, not looking at her.

"I'm sorry," Aria said, stopping to look at Teri when she realized that the girl's smart mouth only masked her hurt feelings. She was as vulnerable as her brother, in her own way. "I wish you'd found out differently. Nothing about that was right."

Teri shrugged one shoulder, trying to look as if she didn't care. "I'm not angry," she said. "But it would have been nice to have known earlier." A few moments later, she added, "So, will you be staying in Itirangi? Because it's not such a bad place. I could visit and babysit sometimes."

"Look who's changed their tune," Eli said, rejoining the

conversation. "Remember when you arrived and couldn't wait to leave?"

"It wasn't so bad," she repeated, her cheeks flushing pink. "It grew on me. Maybe I miss it a bit."

"Your brother and I haven't worked out the details yet, sweetie," Aria said gently. It was true, although she suspected she would remain in Itirangi and he would return to Auckland. It was Eli's responsibility to tell his sister that.

Teri snorted. "You're knocked up. You'd better sort it out fast."

Cheeky girl. "We've got seven months," Aria reminded her. "Be patient."

They drove back to Eli's apartment, and the girls went to their respective bedrooms. Aria slipped out of her dress and into a pretty silk robe. When there was a knock on the door, she drew the robe tightly around herself and opened it a crack.

"I'm so sorry," Eli said through the sliver of space between the door and the doorframe. "I expected them to behave better."

"It's all right," she assured him, opening the door wider. But really, it wasn't. The entire ordeal had been mortifying. Even now, her stomach was churning painfully, and the memory of the conversations earlier made her skin flush with humiliation. For a few brief minutes at the beginning of the night, the glamour had stunned her, but her anticipation had withered when it was confronted with reality.

Mr. and Mrs. Lockwood believed she wasn't good enough for their son, and although she recognized their snobbery for what it was, she couldn't resign herself to a lifetime of scathing comments and bitterness. She didn't deserve their censure, and she wouldn't expose herself or her child to it any more than necessary.

"It's not all right," he growled, edging into the room. "You shouldn't have had to tolerate such rudeness. My parents' manners seem to have deserted them. I'm just so damn *sorry*."

Aria took a step back, disconcerted by an unfamiliar emotion shining in his eyes. *What is it?* His hair was tousled as though he'd been running his hands through it, and the top three buttons of his shirt were undone, exposing a delicious strip of chest. *No, don't get distracted.*

"It's not your fault," she reminded him. "You don't have to apologize for them. The truth is, I should have been more careful. We shouldn't be in this situation—they're right about that."

"I wouldn't take it back." The words ripped from his throat, and he looked startled by them. "Not for anything." He stepped closer, cornering her against the wall. "We have something, Ri. I don't know what you see in me, or why you think I'm qualified to be a dad, but I trust you, and I'm ready to try."

Of all the things she had hoped would happen tonight, this was so far outside the realm of possibility that it hadn't even featured on the list.

"What do you mean?" she asked, in case she was reading too much into his statement.

"You said you wanted us to have a proper relationship," he reminded her. "I'm ready for that now. I admire you and desire you, and I'm not ready to give you up." He bent to kiss her, but she darted out of the way. "What's the matter?"

"You've changed your mind," Aria said. "But so have I. You were right. It was naive of me to think we could work out. You saw the way your parents looked at me. I can't handle being judged and found wanting for the rest of my life. I have more self-respect than that." She inhaled unevenly. "While I appreciate your support, we can't be together."

He reached for her, but she dodged him, putting the bed between them.

"We're from different worlds. I'm a reporter from a small

town in the middle of nowhere. I live in a sixty-year-old cottage, and my idea of a good time is having my friends over for a few drinks and a facial. You're a big-city businessman. You grew up in a mansion and date socialites. How could it work?"

"You could move in with me."

She almost buckled at the hope in his voice. Pain tightened like a vice around her heart.

He stared at her eagerly. "You said you like it here."

"It's a nice apartment," she agreed. "But I like my home. I like being near my family, and I think our child should have a back yard to grow up in."

"We'll buy a house in the suburbs," he said with a hitch in his smile. "We can visit your parents regularly."

Aria squeezed her hands into fists, angry at the unfairness of this. Why did she have to care for someone who was so different from herself? "I'm not cut out for living in the city, Eli."

"We can negotiate. Find an arrangement that suits us both. I'm open to anything, sweetheart. I'm in this with you."

She closed her eyes. It was too much. She'd longed to hear those words, but she couldn't deal with this right now. "What brought on the change of heart?"

"You challenged me to think about myself," he replied. "I realized I'm not like my parents. I can do better than they did."

It was a revelation to him, but she had known it all along. Anyone who worried so much about their reckless little sister couldn't be a total failure as a parent.

"Of course you can," she said softly. She opened her eyes and looked straight at him. "But there's something I need to tell you." He would see her differently after this, she was sure of it. Her belly churned. It was right to tell him, but she wished it wasn't necessary.

"What is it? Is the baby okay?"

"As far as I know, the baby is fine. This is about me."

He didn't look surprised. Maybe he knew more about her than she thought.

"I didn't always want to stay in Itirangi," she continued. "I spent several years in Christchurch, working for the *Press*."

He nodded and gestured for her to continue.

"It was a great job. I loved it, and I was good at it."

"Tell me what happened," Eli pleaded.

"I got a promotion, but some of my colleagues didn't think I deserved it. They decided I must have earned it on my back." She tried to smile but felt her lips twist bitterly. "No one believed I'd earned it on my own merit. I was too young, too inexperienced, and the editor had made no secret of his interest in me."

Eli's jaw ticked, but otherwise, he didn't move.

"It didn't matter that I'd never slept with him or led him to expect anything from me. No one wanted to work with me anymore. They whispered about me behind my back, and it became unbearable."

"I'm sorry you went through that," he said. "But you survived. What does it matter to us now?"

"I haven't finished," she told him. "The worst of it was that the editor actually thought I would sleep with him. He said —" She choked on her words, tears of shame rising at the memory. "He said," she continued gamely, "since everyone already believed it, I might as well make it true."

"That bastard," Eli swore, looking for all the world like he wanted to tear someone's head off. "I'll—"

"You'll do nothing," Aria interrupted. "It's in the past. I've moved on, but I couldn't stay in that job with those people. I had to get out of there."

"So, you went home?"

"Yes. Mum and Dad let me move in, no questions asked. I bought my cottage and eventually took the job at the *Chronicle*. Do you understand where I'm going with this yet?"

"No."

Aria breathed deeply, fortifying herself. "I know what it's like to be called a gold-digger and a whore, Eli. I won't put myself in that position again. I'm not strong enough to handle it. That's why we can't be together."

"I'm sorry about what happened to you," he said, and somehow, he was at her side again, caressing her cheek with his thumb and swiping a tear from the corner of her eye. "But you can't believe I would ever let it happen again."

"You couldn't stop it," she countered, shrinking back from him.

He gripped her chin and tilted her face toward his. "If anyone hurt you like that, I swear I would make them pay." His eyes were dark, intense. Thrilling. "If my parents can't get over themselves, then good riddance to them."

The words were reckless, and he couldn't possibly mean them. If he cast aside his family, he'd inevitably grow to resent her.

"I won't come between family," she said. "The answer is no. You were right to begin with. I'll stay in Itirangi, you return to Auckland, and we can work out the best custody arrangement. We have plenty of time."

Eli's face darkened. "For God's sake, Aria. That's not what I want."

She turned away, and this time, he let her. "I'm sorry, Eli."

THEY SPOKE ONLY when necessary the following day. Teri, aware of the tension but unsure of its origin, occupied herself on her cell phone rather than engage with them. When they dropped her off at school, she hugged Aria tightly and told her to be strong. Aria brushed the girl's hair away from her face and told her to behave. They hugged again, and then Eli and Aria moved on.

A black mood had descended. She loathed herself for having taken so long to realize that she and Eli wouldn't work. Her naivete earlier only made it harder now. They flew back south, and this time, she didn't hold Eli's hand, preferring to grit her teeth and deal with her fear of flying on her own.

It was mid-afternoon when he dropped her back at her cottage.

"I wish the weekend had gone better," he said, carrying her bag to the door. "I apologize on my parents' behalf." He slid her a sidelong glance. "I don't suppose you've reconsidered my offer?"

"Sorry, but no," she said firmly, grateful for the reminder that his family disliked her. She needed to keep perspective.

"You're a tough woman, you know that?" His lips curved into a wry smile. "Too tough."

She stood in the doorway and studied him. Elijah Lockwood was a good man, but, tempted as she was to see what could happen between them, she wouldn't take the risk. She loved her hometown and never wanted to leave, whereas Eli would hightail it out of here as soon as his mall was up and running. His family would never accept her, and she wasn't prepared to drive a wedge between them. So, despite their chemistry, this relationship couldn't continue—because, one way or another, it would break her heart.

"I have my reasons."

"I know," he said, stooping to nuzzle her neck. The sensation of his midday stubble against her skin felt like coming home, and she almost forgot why they couldn't be together.

"We can't," she said. "Please don't make this harder than it needs to be."

"You're wrong," he replied, trailing kisses down the side of her neck. "And I'll make you see it."

"It would never work out," she insisted, fisting her hands in her skirt.

"You can't know that."

The spice of his cologne wound around her, enticing her to rub her face into the crook of his neck. Her legs went weak. "I've got a pretty good idea," she sighed, leaning against the wall for support. "We have completely different lifestyles. If I came with you, I'd be unhappy, and if you stayed here, you'd be unhappy. Your parents don't like me. It's better if we avoid all the drama and part ways now."

"How do you know you'd be unhappy?" he asked, drawing back. Hurt had clouded his eyes, and she desperately wanted to kiss the pain away. "You haven't tried."

"I lived away from here for eight years," Aria replied. "The happiest I've ever been was when I returned and got back on my feet. This is where I belong."

"Maybe you could belong with me."

Steeling her heart against him, she blinked back a flood of tears. "We barely know each other. For all you know, I could make you miserable. Take some time to think about it, and I'm sure you'll agree with me in the end."

Eli pressed a kiss to her forehead and whispered, "Please don't do this."

She unlocked the door and pushed past him, closing it behind her. When she heard him leave, she collapsed against it and wept.

CHAPTER 24

*E*li tossed and turned. He couldn't sleep. Not with Aria out of reach. Instead, he climbed out of bed and wandered into the kitchen. He needed to *do* something. This inaction was killing him. Grabbing a pen and paper from the office, he decided to come up with a plan.

What does a pregnant woman need?

The clock ticked loudly in the quiet room, marking the wasted seconds as he thought of nothing. Weary of the silence and his failure, he picked up the phone and called Teri.

"It's stupid o'clock," she groaned when she answered. "What are you doing up? And why are you calling?"

Eli rubbed a hand over his forehead. "Couldn't sleep."

"Not my problem." Teri sighed, and there was a rustling sound in the background. Then she spoke again, her voice clearer. "Okay, fine. I'm awake now. What is it?"

"I need help," he said. "I'm writing a list of things to buy for Aria, to make the pregnancy easier."

"You do need my help," Teri agreed. "Men don't have a clue when it comes to women."

He tapped his pen on the paper. If she wanted to act like

an expert on pregnant women, so be it. He'd let her play the part. "So? Ideas, Teri?"

She hesitated.

"What is it?" he asked impatiently.

"You called me Teri." She sounded confused, younger, like the girl he remembered from years ago.

"I thought you preferred it."

"I do," she said. "But you've always called me Therese."

Oh. There was a sinking feeling in the bottom of his gut. He thought they'd been getting along well, but he might have overstepped. A late-night phone call and casual use of nicknames might be too much for their fledgling relationship. "I can go back to that, if you'd prefer it."

"No," she said slowly. "No, it's cool. You can call me Teri."

He grinned. Maybe he wasn't as bad with kids as he'd thought.

Teri made a few suggestions for his list—some of them surprisingly good. Eli's heart warmed. If he could win over his wayward sister, perhaps there was hope for him yet.

"How do you feel about Aria?" he asked during a lull in the conversation.

"She's great." The response was immediate. "You're pretty lucky. She's so out of your league."

"You like her." If Teri was going to be a bigger part of his life, and he was beginning to think he might like that, he needed to make more of an effort to consider her feelings. "But you didn't like Victoria."

Teri snorted. "Victoria is a witch, with a capital B."

"You've only met her a couple of times," he reminded his sister, resisting the urge to tell her off for using bad language.

"Believe me, that was enough. She acted like I didn't exist. It was creepy."

He'd never noticed that Victoria treated Teri in any particular way. Guilt slugged him in the gut. He *should* have noticed.

"Aria is different," Teri continued. "She's funny. Nice. She talks to me, except for when you're making out with her—which sucks, by the way. She was my friend first."

Eli chuckled. "I'm sorry." But he wasn't. Not at all.

"Are you going to marry her, or what?"

Sucker punch. Trust a kid to see right to the heart of the matter.

"I don't know," he answered honestly. "I want to spend more time with her, but she might not let me."

"When have you ever let anyone say no to you?"

Damn it all, his sister was right. Eli was a good businessman precisely because he never took 'no' for an answer. He wasn't about to start when it came to the most important deal of his life.

THE NEXT EVENING, Aria found Eli on her doorstep armed with a bouquet of daisies in one hand and a paper bag in the other.

"Hear me out," he said before she could speak. "I know you have a problem with gifts, but I thought under the circumstances, it might be okay. I also thought you might prefer daisies to roses."

The gesture touched Aria. "I love daisies!" she exclaimed. "They're such happy, summery flowers. But you shouldn't have. Did you forget—"

"I didn't forget anything," he interrupted, his expression darkening. "We're having a baby together, so we still have to see each other sometimes."

"Oh." She was appropriately chastened. "What's in the bag?"

"A few things," he replied, keeping the top closed so she couldn't peek inside. "Are you going to invite me in?"

"Come in." She obliged him. "There's something I want to show you."

"Intriguing. What is it?"

"Not yet," she said, plonking onto the couch and patting the spot next to her. "After you show me what's in the bag."

Eli sat and handed her the bag. She reached in and pulled out the first thing she touched: a jar of maternity multivitamins. Then she pulled out a box of crackers and another of chocolates. Her favorites. *Their* favorite.

"You really know how to win over a pregnant woman." She laughed, opening the box of chocolates to offer him one.

Leaning toward her, he closed his mouth over the chocolate and stroked her fingers with the raspy part of his tongue. The hot inside of his mouth burned her, but she shivered. He swallowed, and she yearned to trace his throat with her tongue.

"I want you to know that you're not doing this alone," he told her.

She kissed his cheek impulsively. He still hadn't shaved, so his face was bristly. "That's so sweet of you."

"There's more."

Reaching back into the bag again, she pulled out candied ginger, an eye mask for sleeping, a tube of massage oil and a bottle of body lotion. She laughed again. "You really did your homework, huh?"

He shrugged, but there was something hesitant in the motion to belie his earlier confidence. He seemed unsure of himself.

"This is great," she said. "Thank you. Dry crackers are easier to keep down than most food. And massage oil is exactly what I'll need in a few months when the weight starts piling on."

"Teri helped," he explained. "She said to buy massage oil and body lotion. I think she spent hours Googling pregnancy to learn all about it. She's very excited to be an aunt."

The tight coil in her stomach loosened at the thought of Teri scrolling through articles on Google about pregnancy, wanting to be involved. She was as special as her brother.

"Here, I want you to see something." Taking his hand, she led him to the new nursery. His hand felt good around hers–warm and strong. She pushed the door open. Eli's quick intake of breath told her she'd taken him by surprise.

"Did you do this?"

"Yeah," she replied, proud of herself. "Avery and Sophie helped."

"You told your friends?"

"Just them. I haven't told my family yet," she confessed. She felt pretty stink about it, actually. After all, *his* family knew.

"Why not?" She could have mistaken his tone for criticism, but he looked genuinely curious.

"They'll be disappointed in me."

His grip tightened. "Why would they be disappointed?"

"I'm going to be a single mother," she said. "I come from a family who specialize in white picket fences and happily-ever-afters. My brothers are the exceptions, but they'll settle down eventually. Even Coop." God knew when that would happen, though. It would take a saint to pin down her womanizing brother.

"You don't have to be a single mother."

She caught the hoarse tone in his voice and turned toward him to find his chest only inches from her face. Resisting the urge to burrow into him and accept the comfort he offered, she moved back a little.

Eli released her hand. "I care about you. I want to be with you, and I know you want me too. How can you deny it?"

The idea of a life spent with him appealed to her, and there was no pretending otherwise. But a life with his parents as her in-laws, not so much. They hated her. And no doubt he would tire of her eventually. She wasn't

189

fooling herself into thinking he'd be interested in her forever.

"I thought I made my position clear," she said. "It would be a disaster."

"I disagree," he persisted. "Teri loves you, and it would be better for the baby if we were together."

"I'm sorry," she said, and she really was. "But in a couple of years, you'll be relieved I made this decision."

She sensed him draw away from her further. "You've said that before, but I'm not relieved," he growled. "And I'm shocked you would think that. I know I took a while to come around to the idea of raising a baby with you, but don't punish me for it."

"I'm not," she said in a small voice. "But we come from different worlds."

"I don't care if you come from Jupiter," he spat. "You're clever and beautiful and unique. I've done everything I can to show you I want you in my life, but you're too damn scared to take a risk."

Aria was speechless. She gaped at him as he stormed from the room before she'd had time to gather her thoughts. Her heart protested. Because, this time, she was afraid he wasn't coming back.

ELI FELT LIKE ABSOLUTE CRAP. He bought a six-pack of beer on the way home and made a beeline for the couch, where he flopped and buried his face in his hands. What was he going to do now? The gift bag had softened Aria, but only temporarily. He'd made the mistake of pressing his advantage when he should have given her time.

Should he make a strategic retreat? Rethink his campaign?

Yes. The gesture he'd made hadn't been big enough. He

needed to come up with something better. Something guaranteed to both woo her and show his commitment.

While sifting through ideas in his mind, he opened a can of beer and swigged. The golden liquid coursed down his throat and refreshed not only his body but also his brain. Perhaps he could return to his previous plan to win her over. The one he hadn't been able to complete before she'd blindsided him with the pregnancy.

That's it! He needed to show he could fit into Itirangi and make a life with her, and his previous plan was the first step to achieving that. Aria was passionate about the town. She wanted to stay here and raise their baby in her cozy green nursery with the polished wood cradle and colorful stuffed animals. If Eli wanted a future with her—which he was coming to realize he desired more than anything—he had to adapt. She'd made her terms clear.

Living in Itirangi might be inconvenient from a business perspective, but it would have other perks. Distance from his parents, for one. Eli wasn't particularly attached to Auckland, but a quarter of New Zealand's population lived there, which made it a business hub. Then again, most of his business could be conducted via phone and video conferencing. His second-in-command, Sterling Knightley, would be happy to take on more responsibilities.

Sterling was the antithesis of Eli. He had grown up in a poor neighborhood of West Auckland, then worked two jobs while he put himself through university and supported his terminally ill mother. While Eli had started his company with a wide network of business connections, Sterling had fought his way into the business world tooth-and-claw. The two men, fortuitously seated next to each other at a conference, became friends, then colleagues who worked together seamlessly despite their differences. No one deserved success as much as Sterling did, and Eli had ensured he had all the opportunities he could ask for. The past few months, he'd begun worrying that Sterling might decide to leave and begin his own company. He certainly had the skills and the contacts to do so. If Eli handed over some degree of control to him, he could kill two birds with one stone: keep Sterling around for longer and become less dependent on his Auckland-based office.

But first, he needed to show Aria he could be a part of Itirangi. Eli grabbed his notepad and began to work.

CHAPTER 25

*a*ria sank to the floor and hugged herself. Her feet were puffy and numb, and she couldn't stand on them any longer. Tears poured down her face. Stupid pregnancy hormones.

Eventually, her eyes ran out of tears and the feeling returned to her feet. She got up and poured herself a drink. The glass was at her lips before she remembered she wasn't allowed alcohol. She tossed it down the sink, then slumped on the bed and rubbed her stomach, wondering if the little person inside of her knew what was going on. She'd heard that babies formed an awareness of the environment outside their mother early on.

"Hi, baby," she said tentatively. "It's your mummy. Did you hear all that? Your mummy's got herself into a tricky situation." Oddly enough, talking to her unborn baby soothed her. "I love you, baby," she murmured. "But your daddy confuses me. You want to know the truth?" She leaned forward as if she were sharing a secret with her belly. "He's a good man, and I like him a lot. I might even love him. But I'm scared that his family will never accept me. You don't know me yet, baby, but I don't handle rejection well. I'm kind of a big wuss." She lifted her feet onto the bed and curled into a ball. "Was I right to play it safe, baby?" She rolled her eyes. "Why am I asking you? Of course you think I should have taken a chance on your daddy. All babies want to have two happy parents."

Aria recalled the words he'd said before leaving. He was right to call her a coward, but her fear came from a real place. She'd been judged and found wanting before. At the time, she had told herself that her colleagues' opinions didn't matter, but they did. It might make her weak, but she couldn't help caring what people thought of her.

Even though she knew all this, she knew Eli had spoken the truth when he said he would never intentionally put her through something like that.

Everything was so damned hard. She needed her parents, and it was past time she told them the truth.

WHEN SHE ARRIVED AT HER PARENTS' house, situated in the swampy area near the lake, early on Tuesday evening, Geoff, her dad, was outside mowing the lawn. Although it had been a dry summer, the damp ground meant the lawn had stayed green. The yard sloped down toward a section of rocky shore and the small jetty where Aria and her brothers used to moor their dinghy. She hadn't been out on the lake often because the motion of the water made her queasy. Instead, she'd sat on the grass and read while Justin and Cooper fished a couple of hundred yards from shore.

She inhaled the scent of freshly cut grass, a reminder of childhood summer holidays. Unfortunately, this summer was almost over. The days were becoming shorter, and the nights colder. Before long, it would be autumn, then winter, and by the start of the next summer, she would have a baby to look after.

Wow. Talk about getting ahead of herself.

Waving to her dad, she walked up the path to the house. Before she reached the door, her mother flung it open, took one look at her, and wrapped her in a warm, comforting hug.

"What is it, sweetheart?"

Aria closed her eyes, comforted by her mum's voice. "It's nothing," she whispered.

Donna took her inside and poured her a glass of juice. Geoff finished emptying the lawn mower and joined them.

"Want to talk about it?" Donna asked.

Aria looked at the glass of juice but didn't touch it. She looked at her parents' kind faces and burst out crying. They sandwiched her in a hug and let her cry until she ran out of tears. She seemed to be crying a lot lately.

When her eyes finally dried, she smiled weakly and said, "Congratulations. You're going to be grandparents."

Donna's eyes widened, but she rubbed her daughter's back gently. "That's what this is about? You're pregnant?"

"About two months," she confirmed. "I barely believe it myself."

Geoff patted her on the head awkwardly. "You know, I've always wanted grandchildren."

How could they be so calm about this? She wanted to shake them, make them realize what a big deal it was, but she couldn't. They were playing down the situation for her benefit, to make her feel better. They were looking out for her.

"Is that Lockwood boy the father?" Donna asked.

Aria started to laugh, but it morphed into a wet hiccup. "How does everyone know that?"

"Oh, baby. That man looked like he wanted to eat you up."

"Darling," Geoff said reproachfully. "I don't want to think about any man lusting after my daughter."

Aria laugh-hiccupped again. "I don't want you thinking about that either, Dad."

Donna took her aside and opened a bag of chips, then

took a handful herself before offering to share. "What's happening with your young man? This is not the face of a happy woman."

"We were never really together," Aria explained. "But I think I love him, Mum. At first, I thought he had no heart, but every time I'm with him, I see another side of him. He has a little sister, Teri, who's so cheeky, but I love her." She smiled. Then it faded. "He freaked out when I told him I was pregnant, but now he wants to raise the baby with me."

"That's good news," Donna said with an indulgent smile.

Aria bit her lip and studied her shoes. "I turned him down."

"What?" Her mother's eyes widened again. "But you said you love him."

"His parents are awful," she muttered. "Especially his mother. They treated me like a gold-digger, and it made me feel like one. I know I never really talked about what happened in Christchurch, but you must have heard." Donna nodded. "None of those rumors were true, but they still made me feel cheap. I can't deal with feeling that way for the rest of my life."

"Honey, you marry the man, not his parents."

"I can't ask him to distance himself from his parents for my benefit. It wouldn't be fair." She drew back a bit and studied her mother's face, every beloved line and freckle of it. "I couldn't stop seeing you because of a man. How could I ask him to stop seeing his mum?"

"Sometimes you have to make sacrifices for love."

Her statement shocked Aria silent. When had her mother become so practical? She sputtered. "Shouldn't you be on my side, Mum?"

Donna squeezed her shoulders and glanced up as the door opened wider and Justin and Cooper strode in. "I'm always on your side, love."

"Hey, baby sis." Cooper scooped her into a bear hug while

196

Justin stood scowling in the doorway. "Dad texted and said you have some big news."

Of course he had. Nothing stayed secret for long in the Simons household.

"I'm having a baby," she said, resigned to the fact that everyone in the town would know by morning.

"Congratulations!" Cooper gathered her into another hug. He was the first person to congratulate her. She felt stirrings of excitement. *A mother.* She was going to be a mother, and her brothers had proved already that they would make great uncles. Kids loved them. Cooper, especially. She couldn't ask for better support. The thought comforted her.

"How far along are you?" Cooper asked.

"A couple of months," she replied. "You're really happy for me?"

"You'll be a fantastic mum," he said. "And you're going to get so porky."

Aria thumped his arm but smiled. This was brotherly affection at its best.

"It's Lockwood's baby, isn't it?" Justin wasn't smiling. She nodded. "Where is he?" His tone was harsh. "Anyone can see you're a wreck, Ri, so either you haven't told him or he's neglecting his duty. He should be here to help you through it."

"That's not fair," she argued. "He's been very supportive."

The confrontational set of Justin's shoulders was a challenge. "Then, why are you in this state?"

"I'm just emotional," she said, brushing it off. "It's no big deal."

"I'm going to kill him," Justin barked, spinning on his heel and marching toward the door.

Aria grabbed his arm and pulled him to a halt. "This isn't his fault. He wanted to raise the baby with me. *I* rejected *him.* None of this is his fault."

Her confession took the wind out of his sails. "Oh. Well, then. *Are you stupid?*"

"Shut up," Cooper told Justin. "She must have her reasons. Give her a break."

"It's his parents," Donna said. "She hates them."

"Can't pick your family," Cooper said, changing his tune. "Give the man a break."

She rolled her eyes at his abrupt change of opinion. It couldn't really be that simple, could it? Then again, maybe it was. She *loved* Eli. She loved him for his rare smile, his determination, and his good heart. Was putting up with his parents really too high of a price to pay? What sort of person would she be to ignore real love?

Not someone she could be proud of.

"Coop, you're a genius!" She planted a kiss on his cheek. Her brother, the handsome ex-soldier. A genius. Who knew?

"Well, yeah." He grinned. "It took you a while to notice."

"I have to see Eli," she said, flying out the door. "I love him."

WHILE ARIA WAS LEAVING HER PARENTS' house, Eli was on the phone to his mother.

"You knew what you were doing to me when you brought Victoria to that fundraiser," he accused her. "Every comment you made and every action you took belittled Aria and drove her away. Never mind that I had chosen to date her. You didn't think she was good enough. You've ruined everything."

"Darling, I saved you. Your future is with your business in Auckland, not in some inconsequential town with some nobody girl."

"My future is exactly what *I* choose it to be," Eli snapped, the last cords of his temper fraying. "Aria and my baby. That's what I want. And Teri. Jesus Christ, she deserves better. If she wants to run the company one day, then fine. But that's her call. If she wants to come back and stay with me here, as far as I'm concerned, she can. You know, there's a good chance she will. There's not much for her at home."

"I'm sorry you feel like that," Frances said more softly, and Eli thought that maybe, just maybe, she meant what she was saying. Either way, he had to press on.

"I want you to be part of my life, Mother. I want my kid to have a nana and granddad, but you have to decide whether you can accept the decisions I've made. Do you think you can do that?"

"I can try," she replied, as serious as he'd ever heard her. "If you'll give me another chance."

Eli stopped pacing the length of the room and studied the ring displayed inside the jewelry box on his bedside cabinet. "Of course I'll give you another chance," he replied. "You're family." He was coming to realize that family meant more than he'd ever given it credit for.

"Thank you."

Picking up the ring box, he ran his finger over the stone. "I love you," he said. "I just wish you were more open-minded."

"I'll try to be," Frances said. "I can't promise to be better all at once, but I will try. Good luck with your Aria."

"Thanks. I'll need it."

TERI CALLED SOON after Eli had finished his conversation with Frances. The talk with their mother had raised his optimism, and now Teri, a fountain of enthusiasm, was full of questions because he hadn't gotten around to updating her on his efforts with Aria.

"So? How did it go?" she asked. "Did she love it?"

He sighed. "She loved it, but she still won't give me a chance."

"Oh." Teri deflated.

"It's okay," he assured her. "I have a plan. I've been working on it all afternoon, and hopefully, it will change her mind."

"Oh, really?" Teri sounded skeptical in the way only a teenage girl could—as if everyone older than twenty was inherently stupid.

He grinned. "I can be very persuasive. But if I want it to work, I'd better get busy. I have a lot to do, and I don't want to leave it too late."

CHAPTER 26

*E*li was deep in his work when the door slammed open and footsteps pounded down the hall.

"Not now," he said shortly, thinking it was one of the workmen from the construction site. Recently, they'd taken to interrupting him at home when an issue needed to be resolved. "I'm busy."

"It won't take long."

Startled, he spun around to see Aria silhouetted in the doorway. The tight singlet she was wearing outlined the curve of her stomach, where his child was growing.

"What are you doing here?"

She crossed the room, her smile uncertain. "I came to see you. I've been thinking about a few things. Can we talk?"

She wanted to talk *now*? He was buried in paperwork, doing what was necessary to win her back. He didn't want to argue with her anymore. He just needed the time to get everything in motion, then he could talk to her properly, explain what he was doing and confess his feelings.

"I'm busy at the moment," he repeated, doing his best to ignore the hurt in her eyes. In a couple of days, when everything was wrapped up tidily, then she'd understand. "Would you be able to come back later?"

"This is important," she said quietly.

Damn, it was probably something to do with the baby. A bolt of fear shot through him. Odd. Up until now, he'd been thinking that because he wanted Aria in his life, he was willing to take on the responsibility of being a father in order to have her. But it seemed that, at some point, he had stopped merely accepting his baby and started to care for it.

"Is anything wrong with the baby?" he asked.

"No," she said quickly. "It's fine, as far as I know. But I suppose we should schedule an appointment with an obstetrician sometime."

We. He liked the sound of that. Soon, they could plan for their future together, but before he could enjoy the fruits of his labor, he had to tie up the loose ends. Work before play.

"That's great. Book an appointment and let me know the time and place. I'll be there. But I *am* busy now, Ri." He gestured toward the pile of papers scattered across the desktop. "I need to get back to work. Perhaps we can see each other tomorrow. For lunch?"

She exhaled on a sigh, the movement drawing attention to her breasts. His groin tightened. After he won her back, they had a lot of catching up to do. Then he would learn every inch of her body and taste every bit of that smooth olive skin.

"You can go back to work," she murmured, stepping away from him. "Don't worry about lunch tomorrow. Take care of whatever it is that has you so engrossed."

"I'll call you," he assured her, wanting her to know that, even though he was busy, she still mattered. Aria didn't reply, just inclined her head and left the room.

∾

How could she be so stupid? Aria had known taking a chance on Eli would only cause her pain, but she hadn't imagined he would dismiss her without even hearing her out. She must not mean as much to him as she'd hoped. A man who loved her wouldn't send her away so cruelly. Luckily, she hadn't humiliated herself by telling him she loved him.

Who said that love was pleasant? It was miserable. Her stomach formed a tangle of knots. She felt sick. Her nose ran and her eyes watered. She sniffed, wiped away the wetness and pulled herself together.

Cooper was waiting in the car, and the headlights illuminated the path from the villa. After she'd hurried from their parents' house, he had chased after her and persuaded her to bring him along for moral support. She didn't want to face him now. Holding her shoulders back, she slid into the passenger seat and stared straight ahead.

"How'd it go?" he asked. The confident smile he was wearing faded when she didn't reply. "Ri, what happened?"

"He didn't have time for me," she said, the words breaking her apart. "I was ready to put my heart on the line, and he didn't have time for me. How could he be like that?"

"Jackass," Cooper muttered, slinging an arm around her shoulders. "You deserve better. You know that, right?"

Although she nodded, doubt was creeping up on her. She wasn't special. She was eccentric, plain. Eli Lockwood was handsome, rich, and so far beyond her that it was laughable. She might be pregnant with his child, but she should never have expected anything more. She'd set herself up for a fall, and the landing was hard.

"Take me home," she pleaded. "Please, Coop. I want to be alone."

The drive was silent, and Aria retreated into herself. Once she was home, she crawled under the covers, closed her eyes and cried. If she'd thought she'd cried herself out earlier, she'd been mistaken. *Well*, she comforted herself, *if all else fails, I can make a living for myself as a watering pot.*

~

ELI HAD FINISHED WORKING and was fixing himself a sandwich for supper when the door slammed open for the second time that day. Hoping it was Aria again, he got to his feet and was about to call out when two large, angry men strode into the room. Before he could identify them, one of the men hoisted him by his collar and shoved him against the wall. His face only inches away, his eyes narrow and his mouth twisted into a scowl, Eli recognized Justin Simons.

"What the hell are you doing?" Eli yelled.

Justin dropped him, a momentary reprieve, but pain exploded through his head when a meaty fist connected with his eye. Eli staggered back against the wall, then propelled himself forward with fists flying until he hit something soft. Justin grunted. Eli straightened and adopted a defensive stance. He wasn't a violent guy, but he needed a physical outlet for his pent-up energy, and adrenaline pumped through his body. Justin hunched over and barreled into his knees. Eli rolled over his back and landed behind him. Justin fell forward onto his stomach.

A low chuckle sounded from the doorway. "Get up, you two meatheads."

Eli turned around slowly, reluctant to present his back to Justin. It might be too tempting for him to resist. The other Simons brother, Cooper, was leaning against the wall, watching them with interest.

"I expected Justin to act like a moron, but I thought better of you," he said to Eli. "At least I did until I heard how you treated my baby sister today."

Eli frowned. As far as he could recall, his and Aria's inter-action today had been limited. He'd given her a gift, and she'd

204

rejected him. Then she'd visited while he was working, and he'd said he'd call her later. Nothing to inspire such blood lust in her brothers.

"Are you seriously that dense?" Cooper demanded.

"She's the one who rejected me," Eli reminded him. "If there's an injured party here, it's me."

"You're really that dense." Cooper sighed. He was leaner than his brother, but he moved like a predator, all grace and coiled strength. And he was bigger than Eli. Donna Simons had raised two giants. "Our sister came today to ask you for another chance. Do you understand now?"

Eli's blood went cold, and he scraped a hand down his face, groaning. Aria had come here because she wanted to take a chance on him, and he'd sent her away. She might be strong, but she was also sensitive and in a vulnerable state. "*Shit.*"

"Yeah, shit. Dumbass."

The insult didn't sting.

"But that's all right, because we're here to help."

Eli couldn't help but be skeptical. After all, he'd just eaten a fist.

"You've got to be shitting me," Justin burst out, apparently unaware they were on a mission of peace. "We're not here to help. No way this bozo's going to be part of the family. He hurt Aria."

"And he clearly regrets it," Cooper said evenly. "He looks like death."

"Go to hell," Eli snapped.

Cooper shot him an impatient glare. "Shut it, bro. I'm trying to do you a favor here."

"Oh, so, that's what you're doing?"

"You want a chance with Ri? Stop running your mouth and let me handle this."

"Why are you so sure I want to be with your sister?"

Given his apparent dismissal of her this afternoon, her brother couldn't be sure of his intentions,

"You'd be stupid not to," Cooper replied, staring at him as if he were, indeed, stupid. "She's too good for you."

Ouch. "Thanks for clarifying."

"Any time."

"I still prefer you to him." Eli gestured in Justin's direction.

"Thanks, mate. You're a smart guy."

"Are you two finished flirting with each other?" Justin asked. "Can we get back to the punching now?"

"Have at it," Cooper said, crossing the room to pick an apple from the fruit bowl. "I'll wait over here." He bit into the apple and chewed slowly.

Eli couldn't believe what was happening. He looked at Justin. "As much as I'd love to hit you again, I don't think it would accomplish anything," he said.

"Speak for yourself," the larger man replied. "It would make me feel much better."

Sighing, Eli spread his arms wide. "Do it, then."

"I'm not going to hit you like that." Justin looked appalled by the idea.

"I'm not going to fight back," Eli told him. "I want a life with Aria, and brawling with her brother isn't the best way to start it."

"You should have thought of that earlier." But Justin lowered his fists and made himself comfortable resting against the arm of the couch.

"I love her." Deciding he wasn't about to get beaten to a pulp, Eli pulled three bottles of beer from the fridge, offered one to each brother and took the last for himself.

"Then, what was this afternoon about?" This time, Cooper asked the question.

Eli dropped onto the couch. "Is this an interrogation?"

Justin grunted. It could have been a chuckle. "Don't push your luck."

He plunked himself next to Eli.

"It's a long story," Eli said tiredly, wishing they would leave so he could call Aria and straighten this whole mess out.

"We have time."

Cooper sat on the other side of Eli, so he was flanked by the two brothers. He wondered if it was meant to intimidate him. The Simons brothers might be massive, but he was used to throwing his weight around and wouldn't scare so easily.

"My parents don't approve of Aria," he explained, hoping they wouldn't take offense. "They want me back in Auckland, running my company and married to the woman they've chosen for me. They treated Aria awfully, and now she won't —wouldn't," he corrected, "give me a chance, so I came up with a plan to change her mind. She interrupted me earlier while I was working on it, and I was so focused on finishing that I asked her to come back later."

"You stuffed up there, mate," Cooper said sympathetically.

Thank you, Captain Obvious.

"I don't like you," Justin added. "But if you convince Aria to take you back, and you make her happy for the rest of her life, then it doesn't matter."

"Have I ruined my chance?" Eli asked.

"I don't think so," Cooper said, stroking his chin. "She wants you, but you're going to need a bloody big gesture."

Eli grinned. "That's what I was hoping."

CHAPTER 27

$\mathcal{T}$he sun brought hope with it when it rose the next morning. Aria had cried herself to sleep, certain she had ruined her opportunity for a happy future. But this morning, she was cautiously optimistic. Maybe she couldn't have a husband and a white picket fence, but she would have a baby and a supportive family. She'd be the best mother she could be, starting now. With that in mind, she called in sick to work and scheduled an appointment with an obstetrician. As soon as she hung up, the phone rang in her hand.

Hesitantly, she accepted the call. "Hello?"

"Hey, Ri." Cooper sounded overly cheerful. "How are you doing?"

"Could be worse," she said, looking out the window. "It's a lovely day."

"Someone got up on the right side of the bed," he remarked, uncharacteristically perky. "What are you up to?"

"I rang the hospital," she said. "Made an appointment for Junior this afternoon."

"You're not working today?"

"Nope. Playing hooky." It felt good to be naughty.

"Then get dressed," her brother instructed. "We're going out."

"Bossy boots." She didn't fancy getting up yet. She'd been planning to stay in bed and read a mystery novel that promised lots of blood and gore. "Where are we going?"

"You'll find out soon." Cooper's reply was frustratingly cryptic. "So get your lazy butt out of bed, have a shower and put on a nice dress. I'll drop by and pick you up in an hour."

"You're actually going to make me get out of bed?" She hated the whine in her voice.

"Yes. Out you get. Go on. You can do it."

"Fine," she grumbled. "But I'm not happy about it."

Cooper hung up, and she dragged herself out of bed and into the shower. Usually, she enjoyed hot showers, but with the warm weather, it was a bit much. She hurried through her morning routine, rinsing her hair and adding a leave-in conditioner without blow-drying. Since she didn't have any idea what Cooper had in mind, she thought it was better to be safe than sorry and slapped on a light coat of makeup. She dressed in a blue halter-necked dress and slid into her favorite pair of strappy sandals. Deciding it matched the outfit too perfectly to ignore, she added the blue topaz necklace Eli had given her. No one would read anything into it. It didn't mean she was pining for him. It was no more than a pretty necklace. And if it happened to remind her of their time together, that was her little secret.

Cooper was lounging on the outdoor swing seat, rocking back and forth, when she locked the door behind her. He whistled. "You look nice."

"Thanks," Aria said. "Where are we going?"

"Nope." He treated her to his lady-killer smile—the one that had gotten him under the skirts of most of the unmarried women within ten kilometers. "Not telling. Be patient."

"I'm not a patient person," she reminded him.

"Like I could forget."

He ushered her into his old Ford. She kept silent as he drove up the hill and away from the lake before veering down a side street. They drew closer to Eli's construction site, and she grew increasingly nervous. She didn't want to run into him after yesterday. Not when she'd been so hurt, and he'd been so oblivious. Especially not when she was wearing his necklace.

"Sit still," Cooper instructed as she fidgeted in the seat.

They turned into the construction site driveway, and Aria held her breath.

He parked the car. "Out you get," he said.

"I don't want to be here." She pulled her knees up to her chest and didn't open the door. "Take me home, Coop."

"Not a chance. There's something you need to see, and someone you need to talk to."

Aria surveyed the construction yard, but from their position, only a few workmen were visible. "I don't think so. Let's go."

"Don't make a scene, Ri."

"Fine." She swung the door open, stepped down and stomped her foot. "I'm out. Now what do you want?"

"Walk around to the other side of the building."

Curiosity getting the better of her, she started walking in the direction he'd pointed, jumping in surprise when the car restarted. It squealed across the gravel as Cooper reversed and left her in his dust. Literally.

"Asshole!" she shrieked, waving her fist at him.

Someone guffawed in the distance. She crossed her arms tightly and glowered. Then, without any other viable choices, she continued her trek around the building, wanting to see if she could find out why her brother had abandoned her in enemy territory. Already, she regretted her choice of footwear as she stumbled over the rough ground; she had to stop herself from tripping over loose boards more than once. On the other side of the lot, she came across a scene so bizarre it halted her in her tracks. Her hand shot to her chest.

Half a dozen local business owners, including Mrs. Dodd from the post shop, her friend Emily, and Eliza Brown, were gathered around Eli and a slim blond man. When Mrs. Dodd stretched onto her toes and kissed Eli on the cheek, Aria gaped in astonishment.

What on earth was going on?

The baker, a burly man in his fifties, stepped forward and shook Eli's hand, then clapped him on the back. The blond man stood slightly removed from the others. Even at this distance, he appeared aloof.

She must have made a noise, because suddenly, Eli looked back over his shoulder, right into her eyes. Slowly, a smile spread across his face. Aria stepped backwards. She should leave. She had no right to be here, and Eli was clearly conducting business. He waved her over, and as if they had no connection to her brain, her legs moved toward him of their own volition. She stopped with a comfortable amount of space separating them, but he closed it and took her hands.

"I'm so glad you're here." Wearing a business suit with a silk tie, with his hair stylishly tousled, he was mouth-wateringly sexy, though the skin surrounding his left eye seemed to be tinged violet.

She stared down at their clasped hands, relishing the contact, and pushed her doubts to the back of her mind. "What's going on?" she asked, raising her head.

He was smiling as if he didn't have a worry in the world. It was an easy, open smile that showed his teeth and crinkled the corners of his deep blue eyes. Aria sucked in her breath. He was overwhelmingly male, and she wanted to bask in his warmth. The hot summer sun had nothing on him.

"Can't you guess?" he asked.

Shaking her head slowly, she looked around the construction site. Work had halted, and a few people were standing about, watching them with interest. The blond man was facing her. A serious expression marred his smooth good looks.

"I've changed my plans, Aria. Yesterday, when you came by, I had my mind on business and didn't pay attention to you. I hope you can forgive me. I wanted this to be perfect."

Tears welled in her eyes. She didn't understand what was going on. "I..."

"Don't speak." He hushed her. "Let me explain. I've finalized my plans for the development. I'm going to source all cladding and materials locally and hire local tradesmen to work on the building. I've had the exterior redesigned to match the rest of the township—I even got advice from a local architect instead of using my usual retainer in Auckland." He beamed, seeming sure of her approval. "I've offered all local businesses a reduced rate to rent in the shopping complex. I want this development to be something the town is proud of. Something everyone can be a part of."

"This is fantastic," she breathed, squeezing his hands in return. "But why?"

"You love this town," he said simply. "And I love you. I want you to be happy. I wanted to show you that I can be a part of the community here."

It was too much. She couldn't breathe. Her head was light, and her pulse was thrumming wildly.

"There's more," he hurried on, words spilling rapidly from his mouth and his blue eyes crinkling even more around the edges as he dropped the biggest bombshell of all. "I've decided to stay in Itirangi permanently. I love you, Aria. I love you. You're sweet and funny and adorable, and you challenge me to be a better person. You make me believe I *can* be a better person."

He...what? Was he serious? Aria's pulse was banging in her ears. Hope pierced her chest, lighting it like the first ray of sunshine over the ocean in the morning. He was staying with her. He loved her. The wonderful man.

Releasing her hands, Eli gestured to the blond guy. "This is my second in command, Sterling. He's been asking for more control of the company for years. He'll take over my day-to-day duties while I manage things from here. I'll oversee the new project, and if it works well, perhaps I can try something similar somewhere else. But all my plans are dependent on you, my love." He took a deep breath and looked straight into her eyes. "Will you have me?"

She couldn't believe what he was saying. It was too good to be true. The sweetness of his gesture was more than she'd ever dreamed of, the love in his eyes was real, and the passion in his voice blew her away. He wanted to be with her even though she'd blown hot and cold and had taken far too long to make up her mind about him. He wanted her despite everything.

Eli choked out an awkward laugh. "Say something, Ri."

"Are you serious?" she gasped, still struggling to comprehend the momentous news he'd delivered.

Eli stroked her cheek and tilted her chin up. "More than I've ever been in my life, sweetheart."

"Yes, you silly man. A million times, yes!" She launched herself into his arms and wound her arms around his neck. "Stay with me," she whispered. "Love me."

Then she kissed him. He responded quickly, holding her against him and kissing her sweetly again and again, raining kisses on her lips, her neck, her shoulders. Finally, they broke apart.

"This makes you happy?" he asked, only a hint of doubt lingering in his voice.

"It makes me very happy," she said, then kissed him again. "I thought I'd lost my chance with you. After all, you're smart and sexy and perfect. I'm just me."

He pulled back from her. "You're *good*. Like no one I've

ever known. Don't ever doubt yourself." He grinned. "By the way, I have more news."

"More?" she asked breathlessly. How could there be *more*?

"Teri is going to live with me. With us, I hope. If that's okay with you. My parents have agreed. They're hoping I can turn her into a businesswoman."

Aria's mind whirled, trying to keep up with him. "Absolutely. I love Teri."

"And?"

"You," she said, kissing his cheek. "I love you, Elijah Lockwood."

Eli's eyes closed and he exhaled slowly, a slight curve to his lips. With a jolt of surprise, she realized he hadn't been sure of her answer. He'd been nervous because he didn't want to lose her any more than she wanted to lose him.

In the dusty construction site, Eli dropped to one knee and drew a box out of his pocket.

"Marry me," he said, opening the box to reveal a gold ring with a dazzling ruby set between two diamonds.

Aria's eyes widened. She studied his face and saw he was serious. "Is that a request or an order?"

A muscle in his jaw twitched. "Whichever will make you say yes."

"Yes," she said. "Yes, Eli. I'll marry you. Please get up."

He stood and slipped the ring onto her trembling finger. "I love you, Aria. I want to be with you, and I want to get to know you better every day. I need you in my life."

"I love you too," she whispered. "I didn't want to. At least, not at first, But I do. I can't believe you'd make such huge sacrifices for me."

He took her hands and pressed a kiss into each palm. "As long as I have you, they're not sacrifices," he said. "As long as I have you, I'll be happy."

Aria moved forward until their lips were almost touching. "I want to be a family. You and me, Teri and the baby. I want to have some nights where we cuddle all night long and others where we can't keep our hands off each other."

Eli grinned wolfishly.

"But most of all," she continued, "I want forever. I'm a forever girl, Eli."

"Deal," he said. Then he swept her into a kiss meant to last a lifetime.

EPILOGUE

Christmas, later that year

"*I*sn't she precious? She's going to be a real looker one day."

Aria accepted baby Lauren back from her uncle Cooper and pressed a kiss to her forehead. "My little Laurie-the-looker."

"You don't think we've gone overboard for baby's first Christmas?" her husband asked, wrapping an arm around her from behind.

They'd decorated the house magnificently. She'd strung red and green tinsel across the doorways, and a seven-foot pine tree dominated the lounge. Candy canes hung from the tree, and a veritable feast weighed down the dinner table.

"Not at all," she replied. "I think it's perfect."

"You know she won't remember it."

"But we will."

Aria watched their parents making stilted conversation in the corner. It was the first time Donna and Geoff had met Frances and Phillip—although they had already fallen in love with Teri—and she was pleased to see that everyone was making an effort. It had been her Christmas surprise for Eli, inviting his parents to their home. She'd been unsure how they would react to her invitation but was thrilled when they had turned up on the doorstep on Christmas Eve. The awkward encounter had improved when she'd introduced them to Lauren. No one could resist her daughter.

"I wonder what they're talking about," she murmured, still watching their parents.

"Why don't we go find out?" Eli suggested, ruffling Lauren's fluffy hair until she gurgled contentedly.

Before they could move, Frances excused herself from the conversation and crossed the room. "May I hold my grand-daughter?" she asked.

"Of course." Smiling, Aria helped the older woman bundle the baby against her chest.

"She's marvelous," Frances said proudly, taking the baby back to the couch.

Eli drew Aria into his arms, warming her skin with the hard planes of his body. His eyes twinkled. "Have I told you how beautiful you look today, my wife?"

"Not yet," she replied, knowing full well he had.

"You look beautiful today," he said, nuzzling into her neck. "Would you like me to show you?"

"*Now?*" she hissed, scandalized by his provocative sugges-tion when they were only yards away from their parents. And their daughter.

His eyes narrowed. "Is that a challenge?"

"Maybe." She winked and blew him a kiss.

"Soon," he promised. "But first, we should entertain our guests."

"Our family," she corrected.

And they were. Her family had welcomed Eli into their ranks. They were growing together and making each other stronger. Every day brought more joy than the last, and she thanked her lucky stars for the quirk of fate that had given her a daughter and a soulmate. Forever with them would never be enough, but it was a good start.

THE END

FROM NOW UNTIL FOREVER - EXCERPT

Cooper Simons didn't have the foggiest idea what to do when he was confronted by a harpy wielding a half-empty bottle of wine and screaming. Should he be scared? Horrified? Amused? Somehow, he doubted 'amused' was the correct response.

"I'm not here to hurt you," he said gently. Pacifying the harpy was at the top of his to-do list. "You can put the bottle down. I'm not going to hurt you."

"Then why are you hiding in the bushes?" The harpy's voice shook, but he sensed that she was second-guessing the need to bonk him over the head and gut him.

"I wasn't hiding in the bushes," he replied, taking a step closer to get a better look at her. Other than her wide eyes and shallow breathing, she seemed normal. Wait...was that...

"Sophie?" he asked.

"Yeah?" She lowered the bottle until it hung by her side, her left hand clasping her trench coat closed so tightly, her knuckles went white.

"It's Coop," he told her. "Cooper Simons."

"Oh." Sophie grimaced and shook her head in self-disgust. "Now I feel like an idiot."

"Are you okay?" Despite recognizing the crazy woman as one of his sister's closest friends, he remembered how disturbed she'd looked a moment earlier.

"I'm having a really shitty day," she admitted. "I came to visit Aria, but she's not here, so I was waiting on the porch..." She trailed off, then shrugged. "I may have overreacted. Sorry."

Cooper edged forward and held out a hand, palm facing upward, non-threatening. "Bottle, please."

It took a few moments for his meaning to sink in, then Sophie slapped the bottle into his palm. "I'm so sorry," she said sheepishly.

He set the bottle on the ground, then inched closer, taking care not to startle her. Her eyes tracked him, but she didn't back away. Sophie's bare legs beneath her coat—which only reached mid-thigh—made her look small and vulnerable. And cold. The temperature had dropped rapidly since sundown, and there would be a frost by morning. She must be *frozen*.

Cooper slung an arm around Sophie's shoulders and led her back up onto the porch. He pushed her softly down onto the sofa, and she tucked her feet beneath her butt. Cooper shucked his jacket and laid it over her exposed legs.

"Oh, you don't need to do that!" she exclaimed. "I'm fine. I don't want you freezing on my behalf."

"I insist," Cooper replied, smiling when she stared at him in disbelief. "I'm a gentleman. I couldn't live with myself if I let a woman be cold while I'm toasty warm."

He expected her to be pleased by the sentiment, so he was shocked when she scowled and rolled her eyes. "Yeah, right," she said. "Gentlemen don't exist. You're all the same: a bunch of misogynistic pricks who think with their dicks."

Cooper smothered a laugh, compelled to defend his gender. "We're not so bad. Most of us are nice once you get to know us. It's not our fault we get distracted by pretty faces."

"Pretty faces," Sophie spat, her expression outraged. "Like I'd believe that! Boobs and butts, that's all men care about. Long legs, great. Cold heart? Who gives a shit, right?"

"Men appreciate beautiful women," Cooper agreed, feeling strangely like she was leading him into a trap. "Maybe we let them get away with stuff because we like to look at them. Where's the harm in that?"

"What about the rest of us?" Sophie demanded. "Do we deserve to be treated badly because we aren't a perfect ten?"

"Of course not."

Was he supposed to be agreeing, or playing devil's advocate? Cooper had no idea. Clearly, something had pissed Sophie off. Presumably a man, given her animosity towards him. Though now that he'd thought that, with the way his luck had gone today, he could well have said something offensive and not known it. Damn confusing creatures, women.

Cooper had sought out Aria for much the same reason as Sophie: comfort and reassurance. He'd broken things off with Gemma, a sexy nurse who worked at the hospital, and damn, had she taken it badly. Spouting nonsense about how he used women for his own benefit, how he'd end up old and alone. For Christ's sake, he *loved* women. Which was part of the problem, of course. Unfortunately, he didn't always know the best approach when dealing with their emotions.

He opted for a sympathetic approach. "What happened, Sophie?"

"Nothing happened," she snapped.

"Come on," he prompted. "Clearly, you're upset. Want to talk about it?"

"No."

She said nothing else. The silence stretched for over a

minute and started to become awkward. Cooper was wondering what tactic to try next when she spoke again.

"Men are sleazeballs."

Leaning back against the couch, Cooper regarded her thoughtfully, and Sophie pointedly looked the other way. It had been years since he'd had anything much to do with her. Back in high school, she'd been a fixture in his life, as all Aria's friends had been. The Simons' home had been a popular hangout because his mother, Donna, kept the pantry stocked with home-baked goodies, and his father, Geoff, was keen to put on barbeques or umpire sports games.

After high school, Cooper had joined the army, and spent three years training and six years in active service. He'd been to Iran, Iraq, Syria, and Afghanistan, places he'd gladly forget if he could. At twenty-seven, he'd returned home having seen more death and destruction than most people did in a lifetime. It was enough to make a man sick. Two years on, he still remembered the dust and despair.

In the years he'd been back, he hadn't seen much of Sophie. He remembered Aria saying something about a controlling boyfriend, and Cooper wracked his brain, trying to remember. Hell, he hadn't even noticed she hadn't been around much. All things considered, Sophie was virtually a stranger to him. How was he supposed to handle this?

Sophie snuggled beneath Cooper's jacket, which was still warm from his body. The man himself was as silent as a rock. He sat at the far end of the couch, putting as much distance between them as possible, and seemed to be waiting for her to regain her sanity. Either that or lose it completely and begin dancing around naked and chanting prayers in some mysterious language. The heavy silence was unendurable, and although she knew she had put him in a difficult position, she was angry with him for not saying something. *Anything.*

"You've got that strong, silent thing down to an art," she said finally.

"No one would believe you if you told them that," he replied. "I'm the family gossip, after all."

"Yeah, right," she muttered. "You're the family playboy."

"Is that what the ladies are saying?"

He sounded amused by the prospect, and Sophie turned her head until she was facing him again. Most of the tears that had gathered in her eyes were gone, but she was pretty sure a snot bubble was hanging from her nose.

"As if you don't know that." Her voice had a hard edge, even though she'd meant to tease him. "You've got that buff, sexy thing going on. Add in your charming personality, and I'm surprised women's pants don't magically fall down when you pass them in the street."

"You think they don't?"

His eyes twinkled mischievously, and Sophie almost smiled. "That's exactly what I mean. All you men think about is sex."

"What's going on, Soph?" The nickname slid off his tongue easily, and she liked the way it sounded. Not many men dared to shorten her name.

"Man troubles," she explained. "I'll get over it."

"Vent to me," he offered. "I don't mind being used as a verbal punching bag."

"That's nice of you, but you don't have to listen to my problems."

"Wait a moment." Cooper left the couch, strode out of view and returned with the bottle of wine. "More comfortable now?" he asked, handing it to her.

"Are you kidding? I've got booze and a hot man. What else do I need?"

She was deflecting, and she was sure he knew it.

"Tell me what's wrong."

This time it wasn't a request, but a command. Surprising herself, Sophie obeyed. "Evan cheated on me."

"I'm sorry."

Searching his eyes, she saw genuine sympathy. "It's not like things have been great between us," she said. "But I can't believe he'd cheat on me. I'm so stupid." Choking on a rising wave of emotion, she fought to continue. "Since we got back together, we've been taking it slow. No sex. It was my idea. Tonight, I decided we'd waited long enough, so I went to surprise him at his office." She shrugged helplessly. "He was with his secretary. You know, *with*. And now that picture is burned into my brain. Couldn't he just wait a couple of weeks for me? Was that too much to ask? You're a guy. What do you think?"

"Great way to put me on the spot," Cooper said good-naturedly. "I don't want to be responsible for a woman hating men for the rest of her life."

"Seriously, Coop."

"Seriously, Soph," he mimicked her. "I don't do long-term relationships. I haven't got a clue. I think he should have broken up with you if he wanted to be with someone else, but that's as far as I'll go."

～

Cooper watched Sophie digest his words. Clearly, she needed some insight into the male mind.

"Have you ever cheated?" she asked.

"I copied Michael Portman's answers on the senior calculus exam."

"You know what I mean," she said irritably. "Have you cheated on a girl?"

"I had sex with my girlfriend and her best friend at the same time once. Does that count?"

Sophie shook her head as if he were a lost cause. "You're disgusting."

"I'm a connoisseur of women." Except that after that awful episode with Gemma, he was beginning to wonder: What if all the women he dated ended up hating him? Most of them took the breakup well because they'd known it was coming. Cooper never hid his intentions. Women knew the arrangement was only temporary, but maybe they hoped for more.

"Whatever you say."

She obviously thought he was full of shit, that he was leaving a trail of broken hearts behind him. Hardly fair, but he couldn't blame her, given what she'd been through.

"I'm sorry you have to be here for this," she said abruptly. "It must not be much fun for you."

"I can think of worse things to do with my time."

"Really?" She raised an eyebrow, as if she were daring him to come up with something worse than listening to his sister's friend complain about men.

"I could be forced to watch *Downton Abbey* reruns while drinking margaritas and painting my toenails."

Sophie laughed, her sense of humor returning. "I really am sorry."

"Forget about it," he told her. "Now, how about you get in my car and I drive you home?"

She nodded. *Thank God*, he thought. She wasn't in a good state to drive, and he'd never be able to show his face at his parents' place again if he didn't see her home safely.

"Thanks." Standing, she gave him back his jacket, then followed him to the car. "You're not such a bad guy, Cooper Simons."

He winked, the thought buoying him. "Let's make that our little secret."

ALSO BY ALEXA RIVERS

Little Sky Romances

Accidentally Yours

From Now Until Forever

It Was Always You

Dreaming of You

Little Sky Romance Novellas

Midnight Kisses

Second Chance Christmas

Haven Bay

Then There Was You

Two of a Kind

Safe in his arms

If Only You Knew

Pretend to Be Yours

Begin Again With You

Let Me Love You

Never Saw You Coming

Destiny Falls

Stay With You

Come Back to You

Always Been Yours

ACKNOWLEDGMENTS

First off, thanks to Kayne, my hubby, who had to cohabitate with me while I was writing this book. Thank you for tolerating my quirks, supporting me, and believing in me. Thank you for reading the first draft—even though you haven't read fiction since the Captain Underpants days—and telling me with your unwavering engineer-style logic when something seemed wacky.

Thank you to Mum, Dad, Scott, Shannon, and my extended family for drilling into me from the time I wrote my first story about the adventures of our pet cat, that I can do anything if I set my mind to it. Thanks the years you spent fostering my addiction to books and for reading rough drafts and being founts of enthusiasm.

Lorna C and Carol D, a big thank you for editing and proofreading Summer with the CEO and polishing it until it shone. Thanks to the team at Deranged Doctor Design for making my book pretty!

Thank you to all of the members of Romance Writers of New Zealand who helped me iron out the kinks in my story, and to the SPA Girls for giving me a crash-course in self-publishing. It's a pleasure to be part of the supportive romance-writing community, which encourages people to believe in themselves.

ABOUT THE AUTHOR

Alexa Rivers writes about genuine characters living messy, imperfect lives and earning hard-won happily ever afters. Most of her books are set in small towns, and she lives in one of these herself. She shares a house with a neurotic dog and a husband who thinks he's hilarious.

When she's not writing, she enjoys traveling, baking, eating too much chocolate, cuddling fluffy animals, drinking excessive amounts of tea, and absorbing herself in fictional worlds.

Made in the USA
Middletown, DE
23 March 2024

51973887R00142